STORMY SAT[

Doms of Destiny, Colorado 11

Chloe Lang

MENAGE EVERLASTING

Siren Publishing, Inc.
www.SirenPublishing.com

DEDICATION

To the hardcore fans of this little town I love to write about so much.
Your emails and posts mean so much to me.

STORMY SATISFACTION

Doms of Destiny, Colorado 11

CHLOE LANG

Chapter One

It being only eleven in the morning, Ashley Vaughn walked up to Blue's Diner's entrance expecting to see an empty restaurant. Too early for the lunch crowd. Too late for the breakfast bunch. But instead, when she opened the door her eyes fixed on the two handsome men sitting by the jukebox—men from Chicago she'd dated off and on for over a year.

Nicolas Walker and Sylas Hayes, attorneys for Braxton Meat Packing.

What are they doing here?

She'd broken it off with each of them. Juggling two men was difficult. Long-distance relationships were impossible to maintain. But those weren't the real reasons she ended things. "Sharing" wasn't even in Nic and Sylas's vocabularies, especially when it came to her. She'd believed that eventually they would come around to the Destiny way of thinking. But they hadn't. They never would. *But they are here now. Why?*

It had been wonderful and difficult dating them. The dates with Nic were fun filled. He had an amazing sense of humor and kept her laughing. Sylas was an extreme romantic, wining and dining her, making her always feel so special. When she'd finally found the courage to share what she really desired—that she would never choose between them, that she actually wanted both of them—they had reacted shocked.

Ashley told Nic and Sylas about Destiny and how all types of families were welcomed, accepted. "All that matters is love, whatever way it presents itself. Two men with one woman is not uncommon."

"You can't be serious." Nic continued doing all the talking, while Sylas remained silent, with his eyes fixed on her.

"I'm very serious. You've met my boss."

"Phoebe? Yes."

She took a deep breath and then blurted out, "Phoebe is married to three men."

"That's crazy." Nic frowned.

Sylas broke his silence. "Not to mention illegal."

"Marriage doesn't have to be on paper. It's written in the hearts of people who love each other. Who cares what the law says?"

"I care," Sylas said in his deep tone. "I'm a lawyer. The law matters, Ash."

"What about how we feel about each other? Doesn't that matter to you, too? I know this may sound crazy, but you both have asked me many times what I really want. Well, this is it. I want you both."

"You what?" Nic's face filled with confusion and jealousy. "What do you want me to do when Sylas is banging you? Go get a sandwich or take a walk? When I get back will it be his turn to hit the road so that I can have my way with you?"

"Nic, you've never said anything so hurtful to me before." Tears streamed down her cheeks.

"And you've never said anything so crazy to me before either."

Sylas stated flatly, "Ashley, you know this is not possible."

"In Destiny it is very possible," she snapped back and left.

That night her heart had been shredded by their words, by their rejection of what she needed. She'd been a fool to think Nic and Sylas might act differently. Whatever she'd had with them was over. She hadn't seen either of them since that horrible evening, until now.

There had been voice mails, text messages, and e-mails, but even those had finally come to an end since she never responded to them. She had meant to never look back, to give her heart a chance to heal. But now Nic and Sylas were in Destiny, and the pain she'd been trying to run from was right in front of her eyes.

Were they here to try to change her mind? To start dating again? To force her into choosing one of them? *Not happening.* She'd made her decision to keep her heart from shattering into a million pieces. No matter what they had come to Destiny to say to her, she wasn't changing her mind. She couldn't. It was the only way she had a chance of surviving.

"Hi, Ash." Desirae, the assistant manager of the restaurant, was clearly mesmerized by Nic and Sylas, as she couldn't keep her eyes off of them. No surprise.

They were off-the-charts good looking. They both had dark hair, though Sylas kept his a little longer than Nic. Sylas's eyes were a deep, piercing blue, Nic's a bright green. Their muscled bodies would make any woman weak in the knees, and Desirae was no exception. *Neither am I, God help me.*

"The view in here has improved," Desirae said quietly with a grin.

"It sure has." Anna Banks, a woman who worked at TBK, walked up beside them. "Any idea who those hunks are?"

Desirae shook her head. "Not a clue. How about you, Ash?"

Before she could answer, Nic and Sylas stood. "Hi, Ashley," they said in unison, and then glared at each other.

Their rivalry about her obviously hadn't faded.

"Lucky girl." Anna sighed. "You clearly know them."

"Yes, I do."

"Won't you join us, sweetheart?" Sylas asked.

"One second, please." Her insides were quaking. She turned to Desirae, trying to gain her composure.

"'Sweetheart?'" Desirae's eyes widened. "You know them very well, don't you, Ash?"

She shrugged. She'd been trying to get over Nic and Sylas but failing miserably. The only thing that kept her from thinking about them was staying busy at work. Nights were the worst. She cried herself to sleep too many times. And the dreams, which were perfect, vanished when she left her lonely bed. They reminded her that the real world wasn't what she wanted it to be. Nic and Sylas. Together. Not apart. Not fighting over her.

"My God, they are gorgeous," Anna said. "Don't forget about us if you need any help taming them."

Anna and Desirae laughed.

But Ashley only smiled because she wasn't in a laughing mood. "Desirae, could I have two Blue Plate specials to go, please?"

"Sure thing."

"And could you add an extra order of mashed potatoes and gravy for Phoebe, plus a slice of chocolate pie?"

Desirae wrote on her ticket pad. "Your boss is making a habit of eating dessert lately."

"If Phoebe keeps that up she will lose that cute figure she has," Anna stated flatly.

Ashley was irritated by Anna's comment. "As hard as Phoebe works, I doubt that. She's the county's busiest attorney and pulls sixteen to seventeen hour days regularly."

"Sorry, Ashley. I was just stating facts." Anna was a bit of a know-it-all, always ready to share her opinion whether anyone asked for it or not. Likely, it helped her in her job at TBK, being one of their top computer coders, but elsewhere it was off-putting. "Any of us would slap on the pounds if we ate dessert every day."

"Not Phoebe." Ashley turned to Desirae. "Make it two slices— one for Phoebe and one for me." She glanced back at Nic and Sylas, who had remained standing, waiting on her. "And could I have fruit instead of mashed potatoes?"

"That's a good trade-off, Ash. I'm going to order a piece of pie, too." Anna was obviously trying to lighten the moment. "How about you and I go for a run this evening to work off those extra calories?"

"You're on. See you this evening."

"Ash, don't forget that you might be busy tonight"—Desirae winked—"with those two yummy-looking men, if you're lucky."

She grinned. "Lady luck has never been fond of me, Des."

"Perhaps she will be now. I'll bring you a glass of tea while you wait with your guys."

She didn't bother to correct Desirae that Nic and Sylas weren't her guys. There was no reason to. So instead she took a deep breath and walked over to them.

"What are you two doing in Destiny?"

"We have an appointment with Phoebe after lunch." Nic pulled out a chair for her.

"But more importantly, we came to apologize to you," Sylas added.

"We were both such assholes, Ashley." Nic sighed. "We have no excuse for our behavior."

She sat, and they took their seats, one on each side of her. "I know what I told you must have been a real shock."

"Regardless, sweetheart," Sylas said. "We were extremely rude to you."

"I agree." Nic leaned forward. "You opened up to us and we shot you down. I hope you can forgive us."

"I do forgive you." If she wasn't careful with her heart, she knew she would be right back where she left them in Chicago—open and vulnerable. *I can't make the same mistake again.* Hoping to change the subject, she said, "I keep Phoebe's appointment book. I had no idea you were coming to town to meet with her." She'd thought it unusual that Phoebe had blocked two hours out of her schedule today. A first. Those two hours were obviously for her meeting with Nic and

Sylas. What could be so important that Phoebe had intentionally kept her in the dark? "Is there something going on with Braxton again?"

Braxton Meat Packing had sued Steele Ranch the year before, claiming the ranch had sold them hundreds of diseased cattle and given them numerous falsified records. Phoebe had gotten the company to drop the case because of some records they'd found. That's when she had first met Nic and Sylas, since both worked for Braxton.

"No," Sylas answered.

Confused, she asked, "Then why are you here?"

"Here's your tea, Ash." Desirae placed the glass in front of her. "Your order will be up shortly. Have you gentlemen decided on what you would like?"

"Any suggestions, Ashley?" Nic asked in his warm tone that she had always loved hearing.

"I recommend the Blue Plate special. Today it's meatloaf, mashed potatoes and gravy, salad, and two rolls."

"Sounds good to me." Nic handed his menu to Desirae. "Italian dressing for the salad, please."

Desirae smiled. "And to drink?"

"Water is fine."

"Same for me. Blue Plate special, Italian dressing, and water," Sylas said.

"Separate checks or together?"

"Separate," they said together.

Ashley thought that word meant much more than how they wanted to pay. *Nic, Sylas, Ashley. Together? Never. Separate? Most definitely.*

"Coming right up." Desirae filled their water glasses and left the table.

Sylas's stare made her nervous. "What were we talking about, Ashley?"

"What are you meeting with Phoebe about today?"

Sylas answered first. "She wants one of us to come work for her."

"She what?"

"She has an opening," Nic said. "She contacted me last week and asked me to apply. Today is my interview."

"Same for me," Sylas said.

"No one knows the office better than me and I take my bar exam next week. Why would she need to hire you?"

Nic glared at Sylas. "Maybe she's in need of a new receptionist." Then he grinned. "Don't you think Sylas would be good at that, Ash?"

Sylas chuckled. "I hardly think so, Nic, but you might want to consider it."

Why is this happening to me? "We don't need another lawyer. Phoebe and I are doing just fine."

"During our phone interview, she told me that the practice has grown quite a bit in the past few years," Sylas said.

"She told me the same thing during our interview," Nic added. "Maybe she just wants help to carry some of the load and continue expanding. I'm her man. I will get the job, Ash. Won't it be great working together?"

Sylas shook his head. "And how do you know that I won't get the job?"

Despite the laughs and smiles, Ashley could tell that the animosity between Nic and Sylas was still just as hot as when she'd ended it with them. "Did you two fly here together?"

"We were on the same plane," Nic said in a flat tone.

The little bit of hope that had sprung up that they might be able to be friends again was melting away. She felt responsible for the rift that had driven them apart. They had been good friends. Now, they barely tolerated each other's presence.

Desirae returned with her order. "Here you go, Ash."

Normally she would have paid with the practice's credit card, but wanting to get back to confront Phoebe about this mess, she handed Desirae her own cash. "Keep the change."

"You need a receipt?"

She stood. "I'll get it later. I need to get back to work."

"You got it." Desirae left again.

Nic and Sylas stood.

"I'll see you guys shortly at the office."

"I want to ask you to dinner," Nic said. "I'll be in town for a couple of days."

"I'm not sure that's a good idea."

"Just as friends." Nic smiled. Was he serious? Was that even possible?

"I don't know, Nic." She looked at Sylas, but she couldn't read him. What was he thinking? "How long are you in town?"

"Same as Nic. A couple of days."

"Let me buy you dinner, Ash." Nic continued pressing. "You could fill me in on what it's like to work for Phoebe."

"Let me think about it. I'll tell you after your meeting with her." Ashley rushed out of the diner. She wanted to meet with Phoebe herself, before Nic and Sylas arrived. She needed answers. *What the hell is she thinking?*

Chapter Two

Sylas watched Ashley walk away from his and Nic's table.

Ashley was gorgeous from head to toe. Five feet and three inches of feminine perfection. All the curves in all the right places. Bright green eyes that mesmerized him. Back when they had still been dating, she'd mentioned wanting to cut her hair short. He'd begged her not to, loving her long, dark hair. Ashley was a woman who had a strong will and a mind of her own. She wasn't a pushover, which was just one of the many things he loved about her. But she had given in to him about her hair, promising to keep it just the way it was.

After the breakup, he'd wondered if she'd changed her mind. Thankfully, she hadn't. Seeing her today with the same long, beautiful hair made him so happy.

She walked out of the diner. Just like when she'd walked out from him and Nic back in Chicago, he wasn't sure how to fix the situation—if he could fix it at all. Could things get any worse?

He looked at Nic, who had been admiring her as well.

Nic shrugged. "That didn't go as bad as it could have."

"But it didn't go well." He sat back down, and so did Nic.

Neither of them spoke. The silence was something that had become the norm between them lately. The only time they said a word to each other these days was when it had to do with some case for Braxton they were both working. Nothing else. Ever.

They had been quite close in the past. Very good friends. Like brothers. They'd met in high school and had ended up going to college, and later law school, together. Nic went to work at Braxton first and had recommended him for the job in the legal department six months later. Everything had been terrific for the past several years between them—until Ashley had showed up at their offices.

The waitress returned with their lunch. "Two Blue Plate Specials with Italian dressing." She placed the meals on the table and refilled their waters. "If you have room left after you finish, we have the most wonderful chocolate pie. Just yell 'Desirae' and I'll come running."

"Thanks," he said. "We will."

She smiled.

Several people walked into the diner.

"Lunch rush is starting. Let me know if you need anything else." She walked away, greeting the new customers.

"She's very pretty," Nic said. "And clearly into you."

"Yes, she is pretty, but I'm not interested.

"What about that other girl that she and Ash were talking to? She's cute, and she has blonde hair like you normally go for."

"You know I'm interested in only one woman, and she happens to have dark hair and green eyes."

Nic frowned. "Damn it, Sylas. Just eat your lunch. We don't have to talk."

What a screwed-up mess. He and Nic had pursued Ashley. But she had made it clear from the start that she was interested in both of them. They really hadn't truly understood the full depth of what she meant. So they both dated her. The weekends she was in Chicago, Nic enjoyed her company Friday night through Saturday afternoon. Then Sylas got to see her from then until Sunday when she boarded a plane back to Destiny.

The rivalry grew between them as they each wanted to take things to the next level with Ashley. When she walked out, their friendship was totally wrecked. In fact, this was the first time they'd been civil to each other since the breakup.

Sylas looked around the diner. The lunch crowd had arrived, but it wasn't like any lunch crowd he'd ever seen before. The lifestyle Ashley wanted, being the center of more than one man's attention, was on display at most of the tables. The one that held his attention the most was the threesome walking into the diner at that very moment. They appeared older than any of the other customers. He guessed them to be in their seventies. They greeted everyone as they passed by their tables. The men held the woman's hand, one on each side of her. Seeing how she looked at the two men and how they looked at her, Sylas knew that they were in love. How long had they been together? *I wish I could talk to them and get some advice.*

He looked back at Nic and found him staring at the same threesome. What was going through his mind? Was he also thinking about what Ashley had said about this town? Sharing was commonplace in Destiny. How had she put it? *"All that matters is love, whatever way it presents itself. Two men with one woman is not uncommon."*

Nic pushed his plate to the side and broke the silence. "Let me make this clear to you, Sylas. I intend to land the job. I'm moving to Destiny, and I intend to win Ashley back. She is the woman of my dreams. I am not going to just lay down and give up."

"Apparently you weren't listening to Ashley in Chicago, Nic. She stated she wanted us both and she needed to live the Destiny lifestyle. My purpose here is to find out about that lifestyle."

"Could you possibly share a woman with me?"

Sylas leaned back in his chair. "Truthfully, I never thought about it until Ashley. Now, I'm thinking about It. I really don't know, Nic. But I do know that it isn't going to hurt to find out about this lifestyle. That's what she wants. And all I want is to make her happy. Maybe Phoebe will hire you and not me. But I'm staying, no matter what."

"Without a job?"

"Even if I have to start my own practice."

"Damn it, Sylas. You're pissing me off. She's mine."

"You're barking up the wrong tree. We must respect Ashley's feelings. If you're truly considering moving here, like I am, you need to be more open to the possibility of sharing her."

"Hell, Sylas, I've never thought of anything like this in my life." Nic seemed to be softening a little, but only a little.

"Me either, but don't you think Ashley is worth our effort?" Sylas could see in Nic's eyes that he wasn't as confident about winning Ashley alone as he professed. Maybe there was hope for Nic to turn around. Maybe there was hope for him, too. Ashley was more than worth their best.

Nic shook his head. "Sharing a woman? Granted, Ashley is wonderful—more than wonderful. I want her. I've never wanted anyone as much as her, Sylas. But how would such a thing work?"

"I don't know, but obviously it does somehow. That's why I'm here. To learn how it works."

Nic nodded. "You're the quiet one of the two of us, but you've always been the one willing to step up first when the need arose. I've always admired that about you."

"And I've always admired that you aren't afraid of a challenge. Come on, Nic. This is just another one you and I can master together."

"This is not rock climbing or skydiving, Sylas. This is about the future. It's about the rest of my life, and Ashley's, though she can't see that right now." Nic stood and threw a fifty-dollar bill on the table. His walls were clearly back up. "If you want to get your freak on in this town, I don't care. Have as many threesomes as you want, but stay out of my way when it comes to Ashley. I'm not going to let you fuck up my life, Sylas."

Desirae walked next to Nic. "No pie?"

He didn't answer but stormed out of the diner.

"Did I say something wrong?"

Sylas shook his head. "No. He's just very tired. I'll take a slice of that pie, if you don't mind."

"I don't mind at all." She glanced down at the fifty-dollar bill, and her eyes widened. "He left without his change. You're friends, right? I can give it to you and you can make sure he gets it, okay?"

"Desirae, I'm sure Nic meant that for you."

"That's way too much, especially for the Blue Plate Special. If he comes in again, I'm going to ask him about that." She filled his water glass. "I'll be right back with your pie."

"Take your time. My appointment isn't for another hour. How's your coffee here?"

"Hot and fresh." Her face turned red.

"Bring me a cup, please."

"My pleasure."

After she left, he looked at the table with the elderly threesome. His eyes locked with the woman's. She had beautiful silver hair and blue eyes. The man on her right was bald with a gray beard. The one on her left had silver hair. The woman whispered something to her two companions. The three of them stood and walked straight to his table.

"Hello," the stately woman said. "I'm Ethel O'Leary and these are my husbands, Patrick and Sam."

Two husbands? Destiny was turning out to be just like Ashley had told him and Nic.

"I'm Sylas Hayes. Pleased to meet you."

Sam was the bald one with the beard. "Welcome to Destiny."

He shook their hands.

Patrick smiled. "Since you're alone, do you mind if we join you?"

Both men had a slight Irish accent, though Ethel's sounded American, Midwestern.

"I don't mind at all. I just ordered pie and coffee. Please, have a seat."

"That's why we came to the diner," Ethel said. "We had lunch at home, but that chocolate pie was calling us."

Desirae stepped up with a tray with four slices of pie and four cups of coffee. "I see you've met the Destiny Welcome Wagon."

"Yes, I have." He smiled. "And I'm very impressed."

"Everyone is who meets the O'Learys." Desirae placed the food and drink on the table and walked back to the kitchen.

Ethel took the seat across from him. "I'm sorry we didn't come over before your friend left."

"We want to meet him, too." Patrick slid into the chair to his left. "But it looked like you two were having a serious conversation."

Sam moved into the seat on his right. "We didn't want to intrude."

Sylas smiled. He liked these people. They were warm and kind. "Nic and I will be in town at least two days. I'm sure you'll get a chance to meet him."

"I'd like that," Ethel said.

Patrick took a bite of the pie. "So good. Go on, Sylas. Try it."

He nodded and ate a forkful. "Oh my God. This is incredible."

"I knew you would love it." Patrick sipped his coffee. "Sylas, what brings you to Destiny? A woman?"

"Patrick Michael O'Leary, you hush," his wife scolded.

"Sweetheart, isn't that why most people come here?"

"Brother, just remember it is none of our business." Sam grinned. "And you don't want to upset our wife."

"Don't worry, Ethel," Sylas said. "I don't have any secrets. Patrick, it's partially true that a woman is why I'm here, but I actually have a job interview with Phoebe Blue Wolfe today. Do you know her?"

Patrick laughed. "Son, this is a small town. We know everyone."

"Of course we know Phoebe, Sylas. She's one of the best lawyers I've ever known."

"And that's saying a lot," Sam told him. "Ethel is the county judge. Has been for years."

"Wow." Sylas looked at the regal woman with new respect. "Very nice to meet you. If I end up getting the job, I'm sure we'll be seeing each other more."

They finished their desserts and coffees, telling him more about the town and their lives. It was easy to talk to these three. And he had so many questions that they might be able to help him with about the lifestyle.

"Since you're interviewing with Phoebe," Sam said, "I have a pretty good idea who the special woman is that drew you to our town."

"So when did you met Ashley?" Patrick asked with a grin.

Ethel shook her head. "Honey, you are a hopeless case."

"Hopeless for you, my love." Patrick grabbed her hand and kissed it. Then he turned back to Sylas. "Is your friend Nic here for the same reasons?"

"Yes." He wished things were back to normal with him and Nic. He wasn't sure they could ever be again. "But we're not on the same page."

"Son, it sounds like you have a lot you're dealing with," Sam said. "You want to talk about it?"

He looked at him, Patrick, and Ethel. Even though they'd just met, he felt very comfortable talking with them. "I really must go, but I would like to talk with you more. I do need advice. Is there any way I can meet with you later?"

Ethel smiled and slid a contact card across the table to him. "We'll be home all day today. Come over any time."

Chapter Three

Nic enjoyed the brisk March air hitting his face as he walked around the park in the center of the town. He was trying to clear his head, but his mind kept replaying the night Ashley had broken up with him—him and Sylas.

Damn. What a fucking mess. How am I going to get her back?

His appointment was in less than an hour. He needed to have a game plan before he arrived. Sylas was trying for the same job—for the same reason, too. If he was honest with himself, Sylas was just as capable an attorney as he was. Maybe even more so.

There was no doubt Sylas could set up a new practice in this town and make it. Why couldn't he be just an average lawyer? Hell, Sylas might even get the job and not him.

"Fuck."

"Everything okay?" The question came from a voice behind him.

He turned around and saw the blonde woman who had been talking with Ashley in the diner.

She stood on the sidewalk with a bag of takeout.

"I'm fine. Sorry I said that out loud."

"That's okay." She smiled. "I'm Anna Banks."

"Nicholas Walker." He shook her hand. Anna was perfect for Sylas. Just his type. Blonde and blue-eyed. Until Ashley, the only type of women Sylas dated. That was why they had been such good wingmen for each other. Nic preferred brunettes.

"Nicholas, would you like to have a cup of coffee?"

"I don't have time right now. But thanks."

She reached into her purse and pulled out her business card. "Call me when you do have time."

He took it. "Nice meeting you."

Anna winked at him and then walked away.

He glanced at her card.

Anna Banks. Senior Software Developer. Two Black Knights Enterprises. TBK.

If he could get Anna and Sylas together and they hit it off, his problems would be solved. He tucked her card into his pocket.

As much as he hated to give up on him and Sylas ever being friends again, he knew there was no chance. He'd lost his best friend in the world. He wasn't about to lose Ashley, too. He couldn't give up on her. He *wouldn't* give up on her. They were meant to be together. He'd fallen hard for her. He'd never imagined having a family of his own. The only thing close to family he'd ever known was his friendship with Sylas, who was like a brother to him, but even that got fucked up.

What do I know about family? Nothing. Zilch. Not a damn thing.

That's why playing the field had always appealed to him. Before things got too serious with any woman, he always moved on. But then, Ashley had walked into Braxton's headquarters and into his life. That's when everything changed.

He resumed his trek around the park with its four dragon statues. Now he was thinking about family but he didn't have a clue how to get there. He was certain about one thing. He needed to beat out Sylas for that job at Ashley's office.

Time to bring out the charm, Nic.

* * * *

Ashley rushed into the office with hers and Phoebe's lunches, ready to confront her. Seeing through the glass walls of the conference room, she saw Jennifer Steele with Phoebe.

"Damn."

Phoebe's appointment with Jennifer had completely slipped her mind after seeing Nic and Sylas. Jennifer had been served papers from a law firm in Florida whose client claimed to have proof of ownership of Steele Ranch, which was worth tens of millions. The proof was an alleged last will and testament of Jennifer's late husband.

Jennifer was someone Ashley admired. The woman had lost her husband to cancer before turning thirty. Now in her forties, she remained unattached. She was very attractive but showed no interest in marrying or accepting any Dom's collar. Whenever her deceased husband's name was brought up, Jennifer got choked up.

Ashley had never known Bill Steele. She'd only moved to Destiny a few years ago from Elko, Nevada, her hometown. But she knew he had to be a good man to have won the heart of such a wonderful woman as Jennifer.

She walked into the break room and placed the bag from the diner on the table. Normally, she would've gone ahead and eaten her lunch without Phoebe. Not an unusual occurrence with all the work they were dealing with. But she decided to wait. How could she eat with her insides quaking violently? She was a complete wreck.

She walked back to her desk and could see Jennifer and Phoebe were still talking. She looked at the clock. The seconds seemed to be ticking by at an unusually slow pace. Sitting down at her computer, she brought up Phoebe's appointments. Jennifer Steele was slated for another twenty-two minutes. Meetings with Phoebe rarely went over, but that twenty-two minutes was going to kill Ashley. "I'll just have to wait." Then she looked at the two hours that Phoebe had blocked out after her appointment with Jennifer. In all the years she'd worked for her, Phoebe had always kept her in the loop about everything at the practice. It didn't make any sense to Ashley that she had chosen to keep her in the dark.

Why was Phoebe bringing on another lawyer? And even more so, Ashley wondered why her boss was considering hiring either Sylas or Nic.

Phoebe had always told her that she couldn't wait for her to finish law school and pass the bar so they could be partners. *And now this. What does it mean? Is she firing me or do I have to remain a receptionist to stay working here?*

Phoebe knew that she'd broken it off with Nic and Sylas. If either of them came to work at the office, it would make things very uncomfortable. Was that why Phoebe had kept her in the dark about all of this?

Phoebe was a wonderful boss and mentor, but even more, the woman was like a sister to her.

Another glance at the clock. Sixteen minutes until the appointment with Jennifer was over. Sixteen minutes until one of her exes arrived? She groaned and began tapping on the top of her desk with her fingers. She needed a window of opportunity to speak with Phoebe between when Jennifer left and whichever one of the guys arrived first. She was anxious and worried time would not be on her side.

A minute later, Jennifer and Phoebe walked into the reception area.

"Hi, Ashley," Jennifer said. "Are you getting nervous about taking the bar? That's next week, isn't it?"

"I am. Next Tuesday and Wednesday."

"It takes two days?"

"Yes, in Denver. I will be driving there Monday night."

"I'm sure you'll do great. I haven't seen you at the club lately." Though not officially recognized, Jennifer was considered the queen of the subs at the BDSM club.

"I've been focusing on studying for my bar exam." Which was only part of the truth. While she always enjoyed Phase Four, after her heart had been broken in Chicago, she just hadn't felt like going.

Maybe it would be good for me to go. "Once I finish my exam, I'll be back."

"Great. When does the new paralegal start?"

"In another week." Ashley thought it was premature for Phoebe to hire a paralegal. *What if I don't pass the bar?*

"Dr. Strong is very excited that Erin is moving to Destiny. He's very proud of his cousin for finishing her paralegal degree."

"We're looking forward to her working with us," Phoebe said.

"I look forward to meeting her. We can always use another smart woman in Destiny," Jennifer said. "Thanks for everything, Phoebe. I really appreciate all you're doing for me."

"Don't worry," her boss said in a kind tone. "We'll get you through this."

"You and Ashley always do." Jennifer left.

As soon as the door shut, Ashley stood up. "Just when were you planning on telling me you were hiring a new lawyer, Phoebe? And why does it have to be Nic or Sylas? And are you firing me?"

"Calm down, Ash. I have very good reasons for everything I've done. First of all, you are not fired. I still want to make you a partner. I couldn't tell you until I was certain of my plans." Phoebe smiled.

"Don't tell me this has anything to do with your wedding. That's two weeks away. Besides, you four are already married. I was in Ethel's chambers when you said your vows because you couldn't wait. What's this really about, Phoebe?"

"Congratulations are in order, Ash."

"What in the world are you talking about?"

"I'm pregnant, Ash."

She rushed to Phoebe and hugged her. "That's wonderful news. How far along are you?"

"Ten weeks."

"Ten weeks? When were you planning on telling me?"

"Now, I guess." Phoebe laughed. "I had to make all these plans when I found out I was having twins."

"Twins? Oh my God, your men must be over the moon."

"They are. They're ready for me to come home now. But Doc said I would be fine working until the latter weeks of the pregnancy. Then he wants me to take it easy until the babies come."

"Phoebe, I had no idea. I'll do whatever you need." It was all beginning to make sense to her why Phoebe had not told her about her plans. There was so much that her boss had to deal with.

"You always do. I plan on taking a sabbatical the last trimester and continuing on until the twins are at least six-months old. Even after that, I won't be coming in full time. I want to be with my babies."

"You're going to make such a wonderful mother, Phoebe."

"I sure hope so, Ash. The only client I'm keeping for myself is Jennifer. The rest I will turn over to you, Nic, and Sylas, with you being in charge."

"You're going to hire them both?" *Oh God, how am I going to get through this?*

Phoebe nodded. "I figure since you broke it off with them everything will be fine. Professional. They are such talented attorneys, both Harvard trained."

"Then they should be in charge, not me. I haven't passed the bar yet."

"But you will."

"And I'm state college. They're Ivy League."

"I'm state, too, and I know the law just as well as they do. And Ash, even though you've only been working as a paralegal for the past few years, you know it as well as any attorney. And someone has to be a leader. And I choose you."

"They won't like it."

"When I talk to them today I will let them know that you will be the one in charge. If they don't like it, then they can go back to Chicago."

That would make her life much easier. "Phoebe, I'll do whatever you need. I'm just so happy for you. Do you know if you're having a boy and girl, two boys, or two girls?

"Doc can tell us in a couple of months, but we're not sure yet if we want to know."

"Aunt Ash needs to know so she can start shopping for them." She looked back at the clock. "We only have ten minutes before Nic and Sylas come. You need to have lunch. You're eating for three these days. Oh my God. That's why the extra potatoes and pie, isn't it?"

"I'm starving to death all the time."

"Let's go eat then." As they walked into the break room, Ashley wondered what it was going to be like if Nic and Sylas agreed to come work for the practice. She had to keep her heart in check and stay professional. That's how it had to be if it was going to work.

At least I will be the one in charge.

Chapter Four

Nic walked into the office and saw Ashley sitting behind the receptionist desk.

"Have a seat, Nic," she said in a professional tone. "Ms. Wolfe will be with you shortly."

God, she's still so gorgeous and just as strong-willed as before. "Thanks." He smiled, and leaned over the desk. "What about dinner?"

"Tell you what. I'll let you know after we find out if you'll be working with me or not."

"You're a hard case to crack, Ms. Vaughn." He winked. "No pun intended. One question, please."

She folded her arms over her chest. "And that question is?"

"Will I have a better chance at dinner with you if I get hired or if I don't get hired?"

"You'll have to wait on my answer to that, too, I'm afraid." She grinned.

"Too bad." He loved seeing her smile again. It had been far too long since the last time. "You know how impatient I can be."

"I do. Now, please, have a seat. Ms. Wolfe is just about ready to see you. Would you like something to drink?"

"Yes. Champagne. You and I can celebrate my new job here."

She shook her head. "Can't you ever be serious, Nic?" She didn't wait for him to answer, but stood. "I'll bring you a cup of coffee. Cream, no sugar, as I recall."

He nodded.

She walked out of the room.

He loved her moxie. Loved everything about her.

The door opened, and Sylas entered.

Aggravation swept over him. *Why is he here so early? My appointment is next, and I suspect it will be at least an hour.*

Sylas nodded his direction. "Nic." Then he went and sat down.

Ashley returned carrying Nic's coffee. "Oh, you're here. Hi, Sylas. Would you like a cup of coffee? It will only be a few more minutes until Phoebe can see you and Nic."

Nic was shocked to hear that. "What the hell? She wants to interview us at the same time?"

"Yes." She handed him the cup and turned to Sylas. "You still drink yours black."

"I do. Thanks."

Nic hated the way she looked at Sylas. It reminded him of all the months back in Chicago when he had to say good-bye to her every Saturday afternoon, knowing she would spend the remainder of the weekend with Sylas.

"Ashley, you know more than you're saying, don't you? What's this all about?"

"You either wait and find out, Nic"—she pointed to the door—"or you can leave. Your choice."

Her fire always did evoke such strong desires inside him. He couldn't hold back his grin. "I'll stay and wait, sweetheart."

"This is a law practice, Mr. Walker. Calling me 'sweetheart' is not appropriate here."

"Agreed. Sorry. Where is it appropriate? Dinner, perhaps?" He saw the corners of her mouth go up before she turned her back on him.

"You'll never change, Nicholas Walker," she said as she walked out of the room.

He glared at Sylas. "Did you know that we were meeting Phoebe together?"

"Nope. I'm just as surprised as you are."

Ashley returned with Sylas's coffee. "Here you go."

Phoebe stepped out of her office. "Hello, gentlemen. Bring your coffee and join me in the conference room. You, too, Ashley."

"Me?" She looked shocked.

"Yes, you." The woman smiled.

This was turning out to be the strangest interview he'd ever done. Why would a paralegal need to be in on it?

"Who is going to answer the phone?"

"Let it go to voice mail," Phoebe said. "This is more important." She opened the door to the conference room. "Shall we?"

"Absolutely," Sylas said, stealing his thunder. "I can't wait to get started."

"Me either." He grabbed the door from Phoebe. "After you, ladies."

"Such a gentlemen." Phoebe smiled. "Don't you agree, Ash?"

"He can be when he wants to be." She and Phoebe walked into the conference room.

Phoebe motioned to Ash to sit next to her and him and Sylas to sit across from them. "I'm sure you both are wondering why I'm meeting with you together. First, of all, I've done my homework. You two are highly skilled attorneys. Working opposite you on that case between Steele Ranch and Braxton let me know how formidable you each can be." She went on to tell them about how quickly the practice was growing. "I've got to lighten my caseload since I just found out that I'm pregnant with twins."

"Congratulations," he and Sylas said in unison.

"Thank you," she said. "My husbands and I are so happy."

Husbands, not husband? Can I handle this town and its people? For Ashley, I must try.

"You will both have to get your licenses to practice in Colorado. I will pay your fees. Ashley is taking her bar exam next week, which I'm certain she will pass easily. I'm going to make her a full partner of the practice at that time. You both will be reporting to her."

"What?" Surely he hadn't heard her correctly.

"You and Sylas will be reporting to Ashley."

"Ms. Wolfe, I appreciate your directness, but Ashley? I know she's extremely intelligent, but I've been practicing law for over six years with an excellent record." He pointed at Sylas. "We both graduated from Harvard at the top of our class. Quite frankly, this is hard for me to grasp."

"I can understand that, but trust me, Ashley is more than capable. She is very familiar with this practice and its clients. And despite the fact that she will just be getting her license, she knows the law better than anyone I know. And she is the only person I would trust with this job."

"I don't have any qualms about Ashley, Ms. Wolfe," Sylas said.

Damn, when did he become so flexible?

Sylas added, "I'm ready to go to work."

"But we haven't discussed salary."

"I've done my homework, too. I know you will be fair."

"That's great. We'll work out all the details today." Phoebe turned from Sylas to him. "What about you, Nic? I know the three of you have had a past. But the past is the past. I'm sure that you will be able to work together. You are all professionals." Phoebe turned to Ashley. "I want Nic and Sylas in our practice. What do you think?"

"I believe they would be incredible assets for us."

He looked at Ashley. *Am I only an asset to her now?* "I would love to come work for you, Ms. Wolfe."

"For me and for Ashley." Phoebe shook his and Sylas's hands. "Trust me. This is going to be the best decision you two have ever made. You'll see."

Ashley stood and shook their hands. "Welcome aboard, gentlemen."

Professionalism with her sucks. All he wanted to do was pull her into his arms and kiss her.

"I've got a great idea, Phoebe. Why don't we take our new attorneys to dinner tonight? I'm sure they would like to meet your husbands. Could they come, too?"

So that is what she's been planning.

"That's a wonderful idea, Ash. Unfortunately, I can't make it. My guys and I have plans with my parents tonight. We're going to tell them about their new grandbabies. Ash, use the practice's credit card and get a limo."

"A limo?" Ashley looked surprised.

"Yes, a limo. I want you to take Nic and Sylas to that new steakhouse just outside of town. Have you been there yet, Ash?"

"No."

"I've been there once, and the food is delicious. You'll love it, I'm sure. And they have the best wine selection in the entire state." Phoebe frowned. "Too bad I won't be able to enjoy wine for a very long time, but my babies are worth it. I expect you three to have one for me."

The next hour, they worked out the details of employment. It was quite satisfactory to Nic. The salary was actually twenty percent more than his current salary with Braxton. Phoebe's practice was clearly growing, as she'd stated.

"Let's talk about a start date," Phoebe said.

"I'll need to give two weeks' notice to Braxton," Nic said.

"Same here," Sylas added.

Phoebe nodded. "I'm sure you also have things to settle in Chicago. How about we set your start date three weeks from today."

"That works for me," Nic said. "I'm flying back day after tomorrow. I hope that's enough time to find a place in town."

"When is your flight?" Ashley asked.

"Four thirty Wednesday afternoon out of Denver."

"Same for me," Sylas said.

Damn. I can't seem to get away from this guy. He looked at Phoebe. "Maybe Ashley could help me secure an apartment? She knows the town."

Ashley shook her head. "I'm sorry, but my plate is full, Nic. We have some big cases that I am helping Phoebe on. Plus, I have to study for my bar exam."

"I understand," he said, though he actually didn't believe her excuses. It was obvious that she was trying to avoid him. But no matter. Once he came to work here, she would have to spend time with him. His plan was to make the best use of that time to win her again.

Ashley's tone softened. "But I could get you in touch with Mr. Radcliffe. He's the local realtor. I'm sure he could help you and Sylas."

"Guys, I've got a terrific idea that might solve everything," Phoebe said. "My husbands and I own a little rental house—two-bedroom, two baths—that just became vacant. You could live there until you found your own places."

"That sounds like an excellent temporary plan." Sylas turned to him. "But Nic and I do prefer having our own space."

Why the hell was Sylas being so agreeable? Was he trying to get a leg up on him before they even started?

"Of course, you want your privacy. It would only be an interim solution." Phoebe typed on her iPad. "This would give you more time so you wouldn't have to rush to secure a place. Plus, I recommend that you spend the next two days touring the town. That will give you a better feel of your new home. It's going to be quite different from Chicago, but I believe you both will come to love Destiny as much as Ashley and I do."

"I think it's a great idea, Phoebe." Nic wasn't about to let Sylas get the upper hand on impressing their new boss. "I'd love to see the rental house."

Ashley's eyebrows rose. "Are you serious, Nic?"

"Very. Sounds like the perfect solution."

"What about you, Sylas? Do you think you could live with Nic...temporarily?"

"Certainly. This wouldn't be the first time we lived together, though it's been since our undergrad years."

"That's true." Nic remembered sharing the dorm room with Sylas. Those had been some of the best years of his life. *God, so much has changed.*

Phoebe looked at her iPad. "I just got a text back from my husband, Lucas. If you both have time after this meeting, he can meet you at the rental house." Phoebe handed each of them a slip of paper. "This is the address."

"Thank you," Nic said, hoping to see the place without Sylas. "I'd love to take a look at it."

"Same here," Sylas added.

"Ashley, could you get Nic and Sylas set up with keys to the building and show them their new offices, please?"

"Sure thing."

Phoebe stood and shook their hands. "I look forward to working with you both." Her cell rang. "Excuse me."

Their new boss walked out of the conference room, leaving him alone with Ashley and Sylas. *How the hell did I get myself into this mess? I had a plan to win Ashley back.* Clearly, his plan had to be changed.

"Congratulations, guys." Ashley smiled. She actually seemed a little relieved and pleased. "Maybe this *will* be good for all of us. You know. Just being coworkers."

"Sure thing, boss." Nic smiled. "I only want to make you happy."

Sylas laughed. "Same here."

"Would you stop parroting me?"

"Damn it." She sighed, and he could sense her walls coming back up. "I should've known this was too good to be true. Listen to me.

Both of you." Her eyes narrowed. "Phoebe is expecting you to stay professional, and so do I."

Phoebe rushed in, holding her cell. "Great news, fellas. Lucas is on his way here to drive you to the rental house. What do you say?"

"Great," Sylas answered before Nic could. "That way we can choose our bedrooms."

Phoebe turned to him. "Nic?"

"Yes. Perfect." It was a lie. There wasn't anything perfect about this entire day.

"Lucas, they are ready whenever you are. I'll tell them. I love you." Phoebe clicked off her phone. "He'll be here in five minutes, guys. Ashley can give you the tour of the offices another time."

"Sure."

"I'm very happy to have you on the team." Phoebe smiled and then left.

Nic really did like his new boss. Even though his main reason for taking the position was to get closer to Ashley, he believed this was actually going to be a very good career move. At least he hoped so. "What time is dinner, Ashley?"

"It's two thirty." She looked at the time on her cell. "I have a run with a friend at four. Let's see. I can be ready by seven. How about you two?

"Absolutely," Sylas answered.

"Seven will be great." The idea of going on a date with Ashley once again felt great, even if Sylas would be dragging along.

"Are you both staying at the Dream Hotel?" she asked.

"I am," he said.

Sylas nodded. "Me, too."

"I'll have the limo pick you up at seven thirty." She walked out of the conference room, leaving him alone with Sylas.

Sylas turned to him. "Well? What do you think? Us living together again?"

"It's not ideal, but I'll live with it—or should I say, 'I'll live with you?' Regardless, I plan on finding my own place as soon as I can. I'm here for one reason, Sylas. I'm here for Ashley."

"Yeah. You and me both."

He glared at his former best friend but didn't say another word. Not necessary. Sylas already knew how he felt.

He would keep planting one foot in front of the other until Ashley was back in his arms again. *In my arms only.*

Ashley came back into the conference room. "Lucas is here. Are you ready?"

He smiled. "You bet I am."

Chapter Five

"Nice to meet you, Mr. Wolfe." Sylas shook Phoebe's husband's hand.

The man had a firm grip and a warm smile. "Please. Call me Lucas."

"Sure. I'm Sylas."

Lucas turned to Nic and shook his hand. "So you must be Nic."

"In the flesh. I hope this isn't an inconvenience for you."

"It's not an inconvenience, I promise you. In fact, it's my pleasure, guys. I always enjoy showing my work to new eyes."

When Lucas drove up the driveway to the house, Sylas liked it immediately. It had mature trees and a terrific view of the lake.

They got out of the car.

"The landscaping is impressive, Lucas," Nic said.

"You should have seen it when we purchased it. A complete dump both inside and outside. But Phoebe loved the view and thought it would be a great investment for rental property. We practically stole the place because it was in such poor shape. One thing about our wife, she definitely has the Midas touch." It was plain as day how proud Lucas was of Phoebe. But it was still strange hearing the man say "our wife." Would it ever not sound strange? "We just got it reappraised and we've already doubled our money. My brothers and I worked together on the grounds, but since Mitchell is so busy with his band and Jason is covered up being the county's sheriff, I was responsible for the changes inside. Come on, guys. Let's take a look together."

Sylas glanced at Nic. *Together?* Even though they were standing only five feet from each other, the invisible distance between them was as wide as the Grand Canyon.

The three of them walked inside, and he couldn't believe how incredible it was. It looked as if it could've been on the cover of a magazine or featured on a television show. It had dark wooden floors, a gorgeous fireplace done in white stone with a handcrafted mantle, and large windows that let in lots of natural light.

His apartment in Chicago wasn't this nice. "I wasn't expecting an open floor plan, Lucas."

"The house wasn't like this when we bought it. Since it was built in 1945, we weren't surprised to find it chopped up with little rooms and hallways. I tore out a lot of walls and took it back to the studs so that I could design it the way I wanted."

"Wow. I wouldn't have a clue on how to do that, Lucas." Nic was just as impressed with Phoebe's husband as he was.

"Let's get a closer look at the kitchen." Lucas led them past the massive island in the center of the space. The pride he felt for this house was easy to understand. "I chose black quartz to accent the white wooden cabinets."

Touring the rest of the house, Sylas liked how spacious the bedrooms and baths were.

"You want to flip for the bedrooms?" Nic brought out a quarter.

"They are identical in size, so it doesn't matter to me. You pick the one you like and I'll take the other."

"Fine. I'll take the one closest to the kitchen."

"Great." That gave him the bedroom with the best view of the lake. But did it even matter? He didn't expect Nic to stick around in this house for very long.

When they walked back into the main room, they saw two men, one in a sheriff's uniform.

"Let me introduce you to my brothers, guys. This is Mitchell, the musician in the family."

"Nice to meet you, fellas." Mitchell was tall and his eyes were unusual. The left one was blue and the right one brown.

Lucas introduced the other man. "And this is our eldest brother, Sheriff Jason Wolfe."

"Pleasure, guys." Jason shook his and Nic's hands. "Mitchell and I wanted to drop by and tell you how glad we are that you will be working with Phoebe. Since we're expecting twins, we want her to get plenty of rest."

"That's hard to do with our wife, bro, as you know," Lucas said.

"Very hard."

Mitchell nodded. "She starts the morning at six and doesn't stop until ten at night—if we're lucky."

"But that's going to change," Jason said. "With you two and Ashley carrying the bulk of the load at her practice and us keeping her in line at home, this pregnancy will go just fine."

Hearing the love and concern in the three Wolfe brothers' voices, Sylas was beginning to believe that men really could share one woman and make it work. They clearly had. But they were brothers. He and Nic had been as close as brothers at one time, but no more. How was he going to get Nic to even consider this lifestyle? Hell, he still loved the guy despite what a jerk he was being.

Lucas gave him and Nic each a set of keys. "Looks like you'll be needing these. I'll have the utilities turned on for you so it'll be ready when you get back from Chicago."

Nic was quiet, especially for him. He had a confused look on his face. What was he thinking?

"Do you guys have any other questions?" Lucas asked.

"Yes, I do," Sylas said. "We haven't talked about what the rent is going to be yet."

"We have strict instructions from our wife that you will not be paying any rent."

Mitchell nodded. "She said the value of you two being here is worth a lot more than any rent we could charge you. And we agree."

Jason added, "Besides, the house is paid for, and we would rather it didn't remain empty. Actually, you two are doing us a big favor by moving in."

Nic laughed. It was good to see his friend warming up. He seemed more like his old self. "I really like the Destiny Hard Sell, but—"

"There's no buts, Nic," Lucas said. "You don't want us to get in trouble, do you? Have you ever seen that woman mad?"

"Not yet. Hopefully not ever."

Sylas looked at his watch. "Guys, I hate to cut this short, but I need to get my rental car. I have an appointment with some people I met at the diner."

Nic turned to him with narrow eyes but didn't press him for more information.

"Okay, Sylas," Lucas said. "I'll take you and Nic back. Mitchell, you mind locking up?"

"No problem."

They said their good-byes and left.

* * * *

Ashley finished proofreading Phoebe's last brief on the suit against Jennifer Steele concerning her ranch.

Phoebe was still on the line with one of Walter Steele's attorneys, who worked at a huge law firm in Florida.

The case looked bad for Jennifer, but she had no doubt that Phoebe would find the answer. Jennifer's late husband's eldest brother, Walter, who disappeared thirty years ago and had been declared dead, suddenly had resurfaced. Walter's claim was total ownership of Steele Ranch based on his and Bill's parents' will. It was a solid claim, despite Jennifer's marriage to Bill.

Anna walked into the office. "Hey, Ashley. We still on for that run at four?"

"Yes. I need to work out some tension anyway." Her desk phone rang. "Excuse me, Anna. Wolfe Law Firm, this is Ms. Vaughn. How may I help you?"

"This is Gil Bachman of Neuberger, Bachman, and Minker, Ms. Vaughn. I need to speak with Ms. Wolfe. This is extremely urgent."

Crap. Another attorney of Walter Steele's, and this time a partner of the firm. Phoebe's line was still green, but the man had said it was urgent. "One moment please, Mr. Bachman." She stood and looked at Anna. "Sorry, I don't have time to talk, but I'll meet you at the Red Dragon statue at four."

"Mind if I take a bottle of water?"

"Sure. They're in the break room. Make yourself at home." She rushed to Phoebe's office.

"My client will not agree to that settlement." Phoebe looked up from her call. "Hold on. What is it, Ash?"

"Gil Bachman is on the other line and says it is urgent he speak with you."

"Trying the old double-team move on us, are they?" Phoebe grinned. "Have a seat, Ms. Vaughn. You're days away from being a partner in this firm. We'll just give them a dose of their own medicine and double-team them back." She clicked on the phone's speaker. "Mr. Rankin, I'll need you to hold for a moment. I'll be right back."

"But we have—"

Phoebe hit the button for the other line. "Hello, Mr. Bachman. I'm afraid you will need to hold for a moment longer. I'm gathering the partners in the conference room to take your call."

"Ms. Wolfe, my time is—"

Phoebe clicked the button. "Ash, remember. Just because the opponents want you to jump doesn't mean you have to."

"I won't forget. You've taught me more about the law than any of my professors. I just hope I don't disappoint you when I take my bar exam."

"You won't. And remember, today is your last day at the office. From tomorrow through next week your only job is to study. I can cover the office. Mitchell doesn't have any gigs and promised to fill in until you came back."

Ashley looked at the two blinking lights. "Should we keep them waiting?"

"I think they'll hang up because I'm sure they know I'm on to them. If they are still on the line in the next five minutes, then whatever they have to say really is urgent. That's when we'll talk to them and not before. So I think you should wear that blue dress tonight for dinner with Nic and Sylas. You always look so fantastic in it."

"Phoebe Blue Wolfe, what's really going on?" Ashley had been ready to blast into Phoebe this morning about her bringing Nic and Sylas to Destiny. She'd lost all her thunder after learning about the twins. Though she was still excited, she wanted answers. "There are thousands of Ivy League attorneys you could have hired. Why Nic and Sylas? It's because of me, isn't it? You're playing matchmaker, right?"

"It's because I met them and knew right away that they were great attorneys, Ash. I look forward to working with them." Phoebe pointed to her phone, clearly trying change the subject. "See, both of Walter's attorneys hung up. It wasn't urgent. Just a ploy."

"Phoebe, I'm serious."

"Well, it might work out." Phoebe grinned. "What the heck."

"I am not having my heart broken again. I ended it with them, and that's that."

"Okay, Ash. I understand."

"I know you, Phoebe Blue Wolfe. You don't give up that easy."

"Don't forget, Ash. Love is worth the effort. You know how long I waited. I made so many mistakes because of misunderstanding. I almost lost my three guys. If you're meant to be with Nic and Sylas, I have no doubt it will work out."

"I think since becoming pregnant you're even more of a hopeless romantic than you've ever been, but I'll remember what you said."

"Thank you, Auntie Ash."

"I give up." She grinned and stood. "How can I win with you?"

"You can't. Call it a day, Ash, and have fun tonight."

She walked to the reception area and saw Anna sitting behind her desk, looking at the screen. *Was she on my computer?* "Anna, you really shouldn't be sitting there."

"Oh." Anna stood. "I'm sorry. I didn't think it would be an issue."

"This is a law firm. It's an issue."

"Again. Sorry, Ash. I wasn't thinking. Won't happen again."

"It's okay. It's just been one of those days. Why are you still here?"

"I could tell that last call was important. I thought you might have to work late and cancel our run. I hung around to find out if you could still make it."

"Actually, I'm headed home right now to put on my running shoes."

"Great. I've got to work off that pie you made me buy."

"Made you?" She laughed. "First to the Red Dragon Statue gets to set the pace."

"You've got a deal." Anna rushed out of the office.

Ashley looked at her screen. Phoebe's brief was still up. She closed it, turned off her computer, and left the office.

Chapter Six

Sylas drove into the circular driveway. The house was massive and reminded him of a castle out of a fairy tale. Appropriate, since there was a dragon statue standing at least twelve to thirteen feet tall in the center of the driveway.

This is not just a house. It's a mansion.

He had no inclination that the O'Learys were rich. They hadn't put on airs at all back at the diner. As he rang the doorbell, he wondered how they had acquired their fortune.

Ethel opened the door. "Welcome to our home, Sylas. Come in."

"Thank you." He smiled. The inside of the home was just as impressive as the outside. *Definitely a mansion.* "This place is incredible."

"Patrick and Sam built it for me after they took their company public. Have you ever heard of O'Leary Global?"

"So that's where I've heard your name before. Of course I have. You mean you own it?"

She nodded. "Patrick and Sam started the company back in the early seventies."

"Wow. What an accomplishment. I just read an article about O'Leary Global. Your company acquired Kito Electronics last month."

"Yes, we did. Patrick and Sam were flying back and forth to Tokyo to get the deal done. I'm glad that's over."

According to the article, O'Leary Global was one of the leading tech companies in the world and was valued at twenty-eight billion dollars and rising. The happy threesome he'd met in Blue's Diner wasn't just rich, they were loaded—billionaires.

"It actually started as an import-export company, but Patrick was always drawn to technology. So he and Sam took the business in that direction. And when they did, it took off." She beamed with pride. "My guys have accomplished so much. We lived in a much smaller house in the early years of the company. I told them when they showed me the plans for this place that it was more than we needed, but they insisted. I'm glad they did, Sylas. I love it. And we host some wonderful parties here throughout the year. You will have to come."

"I wouldn't miss one of your parties, Ethel."

She smiled. "I baked some cookies for us. Patrick and Sam are in the kitchen devouring them. We better hurry or there won't be any left for you and me."

He followed her into the kitchen, which was warm and inviting, but big enough that a team of chefs could prepare a meal for hundreds. Patrick and Sam sat on barstools at the big island.

"Hey, Sylas." Patrick put down his glass of milk and waved him over.

Sam finished a cookie and then said, "So glad you could make it. Have a seat. Ethel makes the best chocolate chip cookies you'll ever eat. I swear."

"Thanks." He sat down next to Sam.

Ethel filled a plate and handed it over. "Would you like milk or coffee or something else to drink?"

"Milk, please. Is there any other drink that goes better with homemade cookies?"

"A man after my own heart." Patrick held up his glass.

Sam shrugged and pointed to his coffee cup. "Trying to lose a little weight, Sylas, or I would've had milk, too."

Ethel grinned. "Samuel O'Leary, it's going to take more than just switching from milk to coffee. I've counted. Between you and Patrick, there are fourteen cookies gone."

"I only ate six, honey," Patrick blurted out.

"Why do you always have to throw me in front of the bus, brother?"

"You do that nicely all on your own, Sam."

Sylas laughed, enjoying the banter that these three had together. He took a bite of Ethel's cookie. The chocolate chips melted in his mouth. The cookies were warm and delicious. "Oh my God, Sam. You're right. These are amazing. I hope your wife has at least eight left for me."

"See, sweetheart," Sam said. "I told you we should go in the cookie business."

"I have enough to do taking care of you two." Ethel sat down beside Sylas. "Now, you said at the diner you had questions for us and wanted advice. How can we help?"

"You were right about the serious discussion I was having with my friend. Actually, we aren't friends any longer." He told them what had happened between him, Nic, and Ashley in Chicago, and why he had come to Destiny. They looked pleased when he let them know that Phoebe had hired him and Nic. "But he's closed to even considering the lifestyle she wants. He wants her for himself. That's why we are no longer friends."

"Do you love her, Sylas?" Sam asked.

"More than anything."

"What about Nic?" Ethel asked. "Do you think he loves her, too?"

"Yes, I do." It was so easy talking with the O'Learys, and God knew he needed to talk things out. He didn't know what to do next. "Before Ashley, Nic was quite the playboy. I never imagined he would ever settle down. But after they started dating, I saw something so different in him. If I hadn't fallen for her as hard as I did, I would've been happy for him. Nic had a rough childhood. No family. I believe that's why he and Ashley hit it off so quickly."

"I'm sure you're right about that, Sylas," Ethel said. "Ashley's mother died of cancer long before she moved to Destiny. Her dad then became a single parent of a feisty five-year-old daughter. They were very close, I understand. She told me some wonderful stories about him. Six months before she moved to town, he died of a heart attack."

"It's hard for an only child when they lose their parents," Sam said. "It was good for her to have someone like Nic who could relate to that sense of feeling alone."

Sylas nodded. The jealousy he'd felt back in Chicago was gone. Nic needed Ashley as much as she needed him. *But I need her, too.* "Nic was raised in foster care. He got through college, went to Harvard, and became a lawyer on his own."

"You're proud of him, aren't you?" Patrick asked.

"Yes. I always have been. I had a supportive family. Hell, they're still there for me. Nic didn't have a soul who gave a damn about him, yet I've never seen anyone with more drive than him."

"Sounds to me you're more like brothers than just friends."

"We were. But not anymore."

Sam shook his head. "That's not the way it works, son. Once brothers, always brothers. If Nic is confused, you've got to be there for him."

"He won't let me, Sam. Nic shut the door on me."

"Doors can be opened," Ethel said. "You're both going to be living in Destiny now, working at Phoebe's law firm. You are going to see a lot of each other."

"We actually will be living together for a while." He explained about Phoebe and her husbands offering him and Nic their rent house.

"Perfect," Sam said. "More time together should help both of you figure things out."

"That's just it, Sam. I don't understand this lifestyle either. I need your help, your advice, and your expertise."

"Your head is spinning, I bet, Sylas." Patrick took another cookie, and though Ethel had scolded him earlier, she only smiled.

"It sure is. About so many things. Yes, I wonder if Nic will ever come around, but I also wonder if what Ashley told us about what she wants will actually work for me either."

"You're worrying too much. There are some things that a person must discover step by step." Ethel grinned. "The one thing that can cut through men's stubbornness and hesitation is love."

Sam kissed her on the cheek. "When they love the right woman, sweetheart, it is."

"Can I have an 'amen?'" Patrick pulled Ethel into his arms. "Amen." He kissed her other cheek.

Seeing these three amazing people who were so in love was wonderful to witness but also so astonishing. "Don't you two get jealous of each other for Ethel's affection?"

"Absolutely not," Patrick said flatly. "I'm proud of my brother that he had the good sense to pick this beautiful woman."

"But what about...uh...I mean..."

"Are you asking about sex, Sylas?" Sam asked with a grin.

"Well, yes." He glanced at Ethel, not wanting to insult her. "No details but just how you...uh...coordinate...Damn. I don't know how to say what I'm asking. I don't want to be rude."

"You're not being rude." Ethel smiled, easing his concern that his questions might be offending her. "The Destiny life is very different from the rest of the world. We understand how strange it may seem. Not to give you specifics about our sex life, but I'll answer this way. Sometimes it's together. Sometimes it's not."

"But how...do you..."

Sam stood. "I think a visit to Phase Four would do you good, Sylas."

"Phase Four?"

"Sam, what a terrific idea." Patrick got up from his chair. "It's our local BDSM club."

"BDSM?" He was even more confused than before. "You mean bondage?"

They both nodded.

Sam continued, "Bondage. Dominance. Submission. So much more. It's part of the lifestyle for many."

"Oh my God. Does Ashley go there?" An image of her dressed up as a Dominatrix, all in black holding a whip entered his mind. She'd never mentioned that back in Chicago.

"She does," Ethel said with a grin. "And I can tell by the look on your face that concerns you. Sylas, she's a member, yes, but only a student of the life."

Was this all a mistake? Coming to Destiny? Hoping to understand what Ashley really wanted so that he could give it to her?

"As much as I love her, I can't imagine letting her tie me up, let alone spank me."

Patrick started laughing and Sam smiled, shaking his head.

"Hush up," Ethel told them. "Both of you. He has a lot to learn. Ashley doesn't want to be a Dominatrix, Sylas. She's a submissive."

"A submissive?"

"She's the one who needs to be dominated, and she wants you and Nic to be the ones who she submits to."

"She's so strong and capable. I find that hard to believe." But did he? Really? Sylas had learned how wildly she responded when he held her wrists while they made love. The glaze of heat in her eyes whenever he restrained her had fueled his own hunger. Did she crave more of that kind of play? How rough did she need it? "I guess there's a lot to her that I don't know."

"But do you want to find out more about her?" Sam asked. "About what Ashley really desires from you and Nic?"

"Of course, Sam. Yes. I love her. I want to make her happy if I can."

"Sylas, I think you are perfect for her, and I bet so is Nic." Ethel grabbed his hand. "You two just need a few lessons. That's all." She turned to her two husbands. "And I have an idea. Why don't you two take him to the club? Let him see what it's all about."

"Sweetheart, that's a wonderful idea." Patrick slapped Sylas on the back. "What do you say?"

"I would love to, but I can't tonight. I have dinner with her and Nic. Phoebe set it up. It's a welcome-to-the-practice dinner."

"It's more than that," Ethel said. "Phoebe is playing matchmaker, no doubt. Good for you. Sylas, go to dinner. Have fun. Let the night go where it will."

"From what you've told us, it's clear to me that you three have a lot of work to do before you can be together completely," Sam said. "Tell you what. I'll talk to Zac Gold. He's the owner of Phase Four. I'm sure he'll let us give you a tour in the morning, even though the club doesn't open until later."

"That would be great, fellas." He had come to Destiny to learn more about the lifestyle that Ashley wanted. Thanks to the O'Learys, he was getting a great start.

"Meet us at Blue's Diner at eight," Patrick said. "I like to start my day with black coffee and a good hearty breakfast."

"What about you, Ethel?" Sylas asked. "Won't you be joining us?"

"I can't," she said. "I have to be in court. But I'm leaving you in good hands."

"I believe you are." He stood. "I better head back to the hotel. I need to get ready for my dinner date. Wish me luck."

Ethel hugged him at the door. "Just be yourself, Sylas. That's enough."

Was it enough? Enough for Ashley? And what about Nic? He wasn't sure, but after talking with the O'Learys, he was starting to think things might actually work out—for all of them. *I certainly hope so.*

Chapter Seven

The limo would be arriving any moment. Ashley stood in front of the mirror, making sure her hair and makeup were perfect. She was glad that Phoebe had suggested the blue dress. It was sexy but didn't reveal too much.

Despite having known Nic and Sylas for a year, she was extremely nervous, as if this was a first date. *It's not a date. It's a business dinner, Ashley.*

She'd kept reminding herself of that since Phoebe set it up, but her mind wouldn't settle down. She'd even cracked some of her law books after her run with Anna, hoping to focus on anything but her two sexy lawyers from Chicago. Before their arrival, studying for the bar exam these past months had been the only thing able to get her thoughts off of her broken heart—but not tonight. Nothing was working. Since seeing Nic and Sylas at Blue's Diner, images of them making love to her together played over and over in her head. *I should strangle Phoebe for putting me in this situation.*

How was the evening going to go? She'd dated both men, but had never been out with them together. The fact that they weren't getting along was making her very uneasy. She needed to make things crystal clear to them from the outset, especially since she was going to be working with them every day. But how, since it wasn't even crystal clear to her? Whenever she was around them her thoughts got jumbled and her body got warm.

Damn. I'm never going to get over this with them right in my face day in and day out.

A knock on the door pulled her back to the here and now. *Ready or not, this date is about to begin, Ashley Vaughn.*

When the driver pulled the limo in front of the Dream Hotel, she saw Nic and Sylas standing by the circular drive. They looked so handsome.

The driver opened the door.

Sylas got in next to her. "You look gorgeous."

"Thank you. You look very handsome yourself."

Nic walked around the limo, opened the door himself, and slid in on the other side. "Sweetheart, you look absolutely beautiful."

"And you look absolutely handsome. We must be the three most beautiful people in Destiny." She laughed, trying to tamp down her anxiety.

Nic laughed and Sylas smiled.

"I don't know about you two, but I'm starving," Nic said.

"Actually, I'm not that hungry." Sylas patted his own stomach. "I ate a bunch of Ethel O'Leary's chocolate chip cookies before I got back to the hotel."

She turned to him. "Was that who you had the appointment with after your meeting with Phoebe?"

"Her and her husbands, Sam and Patrick. I will be meeting with Patrick and Sam in the morning."

"O'Leary? As in O'Leary Global?" Nic asked him.

"Yes. They're the founders and owners."

"I saw the O'Leary building when I was walking around the park earlier. It has to be the tallest in town."

"It is," she told them. "O'Leary Tower is ten stories. TBK, the building next to it, is nine. The O'Learys are very nice people. They love the town and have some of the best parties I've ever been to."

"That's what I hear," Sylas said. "They made me promise to come to the next event. What did they call it?"

"Dragon Week. The big party is at the end, which is called Dragon Day. You'll love it." She turned to Nic. "You will, too.

Patrick tells stories about his encounters with dragons. It's quite riveting. Everyone in town goes. It's in two weeks."

"Then I will definitely be attending," he said. "Sounds fun."

Seeing him and Sylas so at ease shocked her. They had been quite the opposite earlier at the office.

"How far is this steakhouse?" Sylas asked as the limo crossed the Silver Spoon Bridge.

"Not far. Just out of town. Fifteen minute drive from the city limits, which we are passing now."

The driver turned left onto Highway F. They rode in silence for a few miles. Had she been wrong about them? Was their civility just a mask for the angry storm to come, a storm she had seen firsthand back in Chicago? *How am I going to make it through the rest of this evening?*

She was about to break the silence, but didn't have to when Nic did it for her.

"Sylas, did you know the O'Learys before coming to Destiny?"

"No. You saw them at the diner. They came in after Ashley left."

"The older folks? The two men and woman?"

Sylas nodded. "After you left they asked to join me. Terrific people."

"Yes, they are," she said.

"What I've seen so far about this town," he went on, "it seems everyone is ready to welcome newcomers with open arms."

She grinned. "That's why I love it here so much. I'm sure you both will too before long."

"I agree, don't you, Nic?" Sylas leaned in closer, his arm grazing hers, sending a spark up and down her body.

Nic's eyes never left hers, making her warm and want to squirm. "I sure do. I can't wait to get settled in."

"We're here."

The limo parked in front of the entrance. Nic and Sylas exited the vehicle. Sylas held the door for her as Nic came around. Gone was the belligerence between them. They were no longer combative, each trying to win more of her attention. They seemed to not only be getting along but were actually working together to make sure she had a good time. *Don't fool yourself into hoping for the dream again. It's never going to happen.*

She got out of the car, taking a deep breath of air. "Shall we?"

"We shall." Sylas offered her his arm.

Nic seemed unmoved by the gesture. How was this possible? Had they changed so much since she last saw them? She took Sylas's arm and then gestured to Nic that she wanted his as well.

He smiled and offered his arm.

She walked into the Colorado Skies Steakhouse between the two men who not only held her arms but her heart as well. She needed to resist opening up to them. She should be stronger, tough even. But she couldn't find it in herself to put up her walls again. They were acting civil. More than that, they seemed to be actually enjoying each other's company. Was it really true? Or was it just a delusion of her own making?

"Nice place, Ashley," Nic said.

"It sure is." She glanced around the spacious place. Its high-end décor didn't intimidate but actually was inviting.

Warm earthy tones and exceptional lighting welcomed them. A long wall of floor-to-ceiling glass allowed diners to see the mountain range behind the restaurant.

A young woman wearing a black dress stood behind a desk.

"Welcome to Colorado Skies. What name is the reservation under?"

"Reservation for three," Ashley told her, "under Vaughn."

The woman looked down at her computer screen. "Yes. Here you are. Vaughn, party of three. Excellent."

A waiter walked over.

"If you'll follow Adam, he will take you to your table. Enjoy your dinner."

Adam led them to what she guessed was likely one of the best tables in the entire restaurant. It certainly appeared so. The table sat in in a quiet corner, far from the entrance and the kitchen and with an unobstructed view to the outside, which at present was stunning. The entire mountain range was illuminated in a soft glow from the beams of the night's full moon. To her it looked magical, which wasn't a good thing, especially considering how mixed up she was about this entire evening.

Adam filled their water glasses and told them the night's specials.

Nic turned to Sylas. "Since Ashley loves scallops as much as you do, I think that should be our appetizer."

How had Nic remembered that about her? She'd only told him once when he'd taken her to that wonderful seafood restaurant on Lake Shore Drive.

Sylas nodded. "And an order of bruschetta for you, Nic, since you're not that fond of seafood."

"Thanks, buddy."

Buddy? She hadn't heard Nic or Sylas call each other that since she started dating them. That's when things seemed to have soured between them. Now, they were acting as if they'd mended their differences. Maybe the breakup had served to heal their rift. But that didn't make any sense. They'd been just as uptight with each other at the diner, and then later at Phoebe's offices. What had changed since then?

Another man, who looked to be about the same age as their waiter, came to their table.

Adam introduced him. "This is Mr. Brett Saxton. He is your sommelier for the evening."

"Thank you, Adam." Brett had a distinct British accent, which was rarely heard in this part of Colorado. He turned to them and smiled. "Welcome."

Sylas, being more knowledgeable about wine than either Nic or her, addressed the sommelier.

Nic leaned over and whispered to her. "Sylas has always been great at picking wine."

"I believe Sauvignon Blanc would pair best with our scallops," Sylas told the wine expert.

"Very good, sir. I have a wonderful bottle from New Zealand that has crisp floral notes with hints of oak." The man held out the wine list for Sylas to read, pointing to the selection.

"Perfect. Let's start with that."

After Adam and the sommelier left, she turned to Nic and Sylas. "Quite the place Phoebe sent us to, don't you think?"

"Very nice," Nic said. "And I don't know about you and Sylas, but I'm glad that the boss is picking up the check instead of us."

Sylas laughed. "I agree. Phoebe certainly knows how to impress, doesn't she?"

"Yes, she does." Ashley couldn't get over how friendly they were being with each other. *What is going on?*

The mood never changed between the two guys as the three of them ate the delicious food. Sylas selected a bottle for each course, but she only sampled one glass from each. Any more, and they would have to carry her out. But would being carried out by Nic and Sylas really be a bad thing? She grinned.

Nic looked up from his plate. "What's so funny, Ashley?"

"Nothing at all. Just having a good time."

"She's not telling the entire truth, Nic," Sylas said. "Can you tell?"

"I sure can." Nic smiled. "What's going on in that pretty little head of yours, sweetheart?"

She pushed her empty glass to the side. "I was picturing you two having to carry me out of here if I drank any more wine."

"In that case." Sylas filled her glass and pushed it back to her. With a wicked wink, he said, "Have some more."

"No way are you getting me drunk." She smiled and pushed the glass to the center of the table. "In fact, I wouldn't mind having dessert and coffee." She knew that the little buzz she was feeling would vanish with the help of chocolate and caffeine.

"Sounds good to me," Sylas said. "How about you?"

"Same, but I'm not letting this wine go to waste. The practice paid for it." Nic took her glass and downed the contents. With a devilish grin, he pretended to be smashed, slurring, "You ann Ashkey be sssure ta let our bossss know dat I didn't sssquander a sssingle drop."

She and Sylas roared.

Reminiscent of their past friendship, Sylas and Nic continued joking with each other all the way through dessert.

"God, I wish this night wouldn't have to end. It's been so much fun."

Nic looked down, which caused her heart to skip a beat. *What is he thinking? Did I say something wrong?*

She looked at Sylas.

"No, sweetheart. Nic and I are having a wonderful time, too. Aren't we, buddy?"

He nodded and grinned, making her feel better. "We sure are."

* * * *

Nic grabbed Ashley's hand, enjoying the feel of her delicate fingers. "This is the best night I've had in forever, sweetheart. But unfortunately you have your bar exam to study for and Sylas has his meeting with the O'Learys in the morning. Maybe when he and I get back from Chicago, we can do this again."

"I'd like that." The softness of her tone drove him wild. "How about you, Sylas? Shall you, Nic, and I have a sequel dinner date?"

"Absolutely, we will." Sylas seemed genuine.

Nic smiled, though his insides tightened with jealousy. *She's mine, buddy. Mine alone. You'll see.* But he wasn't about to show his true feelings. That would definitely be a mistake. He wanted Ashley to continuing enjoying herself, despite his renewed resentment that Sylas was here, too. Seeing her smile and hearing her laugh had made Nic so happy. It was worth all the effort. Hell, even joking with Sylas had made this evening fun. Nic had begun the night with the intent of showing Ashley that between him and Sylas, he was the one who could be cordial and friendly. But the role he'd chosen for himself faded fast as he relaxed into the camaraderie he and Sylas once shared. But their friendship could never be again unless his old friend was willing to stop pursuing Ashley.

Chapter Eight

Ashley said her good-byes to Nic and Sylas at the front of the hotel. "Thank you for a wonderful evening. I can honestly say it went so much better than I imagined."

"For me, too," Sylas said, hugging her. "I'll call you tomorrow. Maybe the three of us could have dinner again."

"That would be wonderful. We have a terrific Chinese restaurant I believe you both would like."

"Then that's settled," Nic said, pulling her in for a squeeze. "Chinese tomorrow. The three of us. You need to study, Ashley, so we will make it a quick meal, okay?"

"I do. I have at least a couple of hours of reading ahead of me tonight."

"Then Nic's right, Ashley. Go study. We'll see you tomorrow."

"Night, guys."

"Goodnight," they said in unison.

She walked back to the limo. The driver held the door for her. She got inside, and he closed it. As they drove away, she watched Nic and Sylas walk into the Dream Hotel together.

Still warm from the effect of the wine and from being so close to the men of her dreams, Ashley melted back into the seat. *Did tonight really happen?* She still couldn't quite believe it. She reminded herself that she had cried herself to sleep many times since the breakup. Was it worth the risk to open her heart again to them in the hopes they would understand the Destiny way of life? *More than that.* Would Nic and Sylas actually want to live the Destiny way of life with her?

The driver pulled up to her apartment and opened the door for her.

"Thank you." She handed him a generous tip.

"Thank you, Ms. Vaughn."

She walked to the security gate and typed in her code on the keypad. The metallic click let her know it was unlocked. She went through it onto the grounds of the Wild Oaks Apartments. The complex was made up of six buildings, each with eight apartments, four at ground level and four above. Ashley's place sat in the middle of the complex, apartment 3, building C. The fencing around Wild Oaks had been added after Cindy Trollinger, the town's nemesis, blew up the Silver Spoon Bridge. Some of the residents didn't like the fence, while for others it made them feel safer. She didn't mind either way.

She headed up the sidewalk and heard the metallic noise from the gate. It was late, but since many of the residents were computer analysts who worked at O'Leary Global and TBK, they kept unusual hours. She liked her neighbors very much, though they did take a little getting to know. Brilliant people could come off as odd.

She turned around to see which neighbor was coming through the security gate. "Hi, Anna. You're out late. I should have known you would go back to work after our run."

"I just needed to finish some coding I was working on. But I'm not the only one out late." Anna grinned. "How did the date go with the two hot Chicago attorneys?"

"It went well, I think."

"Think?" Anna stepped next to her. "By the look on your face, I can tell it went very well."

"Hello, ladies." Henry Underwood, her next-door neighbor, stood outside his apartment, smoking a cigarette. He was a very close family friend of Nicole Coleman, one of the county's deputy sheriffs. Henry was a retired Chicago police officer and had been Nicole's mentor.

Anna waved at him.

"Hi, Henry," Ashley said. "How are you doing?"

"Doing great. I hope you girls are doing good, too." He put out his cigarette and walked back into his apartment.

Anna turned back to her. "How about I grab a bottle of wine I have at my place and I come over to yours and we talk about it? I want more details."

"I wish I could, but I really need to study."

"The bar exam. Right. Another time."

"Absolutely."

Anna nodded and turned down the path that led to building F, which sat at the back of the property, where Anna's apartment was located.

Ashley unlocked the door to her apartment. Once inside, she kicked off her stilettos and started unzipping her dress as she walked to her bedroom. Stripping out of her bra and thong, she put on her most comfy pajamas. She wanted to get in at least three or four hours of studying before calling it a night. Since she didn't have to go into the office, it wasn't going to be an issue if she slept in.

She grabbed the study guide with the practice questions, stepped into her kitchen, and put on a pot of coffee. Returning to her sofa, she placed her feet on the footstool and opened the book, but instead of reading, she just stared at the words. Her thoughts wouldn't let go of replaying the night's events.

She smiled and took a sip of coffee. "No matter how much fun I had with Nic and Sylas, I have to get down to business."

She'd worked too hard to blow the bar. Phoebe was counting on her, and she wasn't about to let her down. With her mind put in check, she dove into her studies.

Thirty minutes later, Ashley heard a knock on her door.

Anna? The woman could be pushy at times.

Ashley went to the door and looked out the peephole. The person she saw wasn't Anna. It was Nic.

She opened the door. "Hi. What are you doing here?"

How did he get past the security gate? Probably just followed another tenant inside the property.

He no longer wore a suit and tie but was dressed in jeans and a black T-shirt, still looking so mouth-watering good.

"I couldn't sleep. Thought you might like a study partner."

"But that would be so boring for you, Nic."

"Not at all. I love the law and a good lawyer never stops refreshing his mind—or *her* mind."

"How can I turn down a Harvard grad's offer like that?" She smiled. "Come in. Please. I just put on a fresh pot of coffee." As if on cue, she heard the maker beep. "In fact, it just finished brewing. Would you like a cup?"

"Since this is likely going to be an all-nighter, I most definitely would like a cup."

All-nighter? Did Nic plan on staying until the morning? The idea that he might want to made her a little nervous and excited at the same time. *Stop it, Ashley. He only wants to help you study.*

Sitting on the sofa, sipping their coffee, Nic took the book and started quizzing her.

Jittery at first because of how knowledgeable he was, she still answered every question correctly.

An hour later, Nic closed the book and grabbed her hands. "Sweetheart, you are more than ready for the exam. I have little doubt that you will ace it."

"Ace it?" She shook her head. "I just want to pass."

"You will. I just know it." He stared at her with his forest-green eyes, making her tingle.

"Thank you for believing in me." Unable to look away, she leaned in and kissed him on the cheek. "I really am glad you came over tonight to help me study."

"Me, too." He pulled her in close and pressed his mouth to hers.

With not even a drop of hesitation left inside her, she melted into the kiss, enjoying the taste of him on her lips again. She felt him touch her breasts, and a shiver ran up and down her spine. The right thing to do was to put the brakes on, but her body wasn't listening to reason. Being in his arms again felt so good, so familiar. She'd missed this so much.

He deepened the kiss, tangling his tongue with hers. Happy memories of her time with him flooded her mind as his hands roamed over her body.

He removed her PJ top, exposing her naked breasts. When he brushed her nipples with his fingers, a spark shot through her, igniting her desires for him that had been pushed down for the past couple of months. There was no possible way for her to stop now. She had to have him inside her. It had been too long. Burning from head to toe with want, she pulled his T-shirt off of him and tossed it to the coffee table.

He caressed her breasts and licked her neck. The pressure began to build inside her. She was crazed with thirst, and he was the only drink that could satisfy her need. He moved down and began licking her breasts, applying just the right touch, setting her on fire even more. When he captured one of her nipples between his teeth, he reached down and removed her PJ bottoms. With only caresses, he guided her to stretch out on the sofa. She obeyed his silent command willingly. He stripped out of his boots and jeans, placing them next to his discarded T-shirt on the coffee table. She stole a quick glance at his cock, which she knew intimately. He was rock hard, every inch of him.

He climbed on top of her, pinning her down to the sofa. She could feel the moisture between her thighs.

After laving her breasts, he kissed his way down her body to her pussy. She reacted like a wild woman, thrashing under him, totally out of control. He ran his tongue over her wet folds before circling her clit. The sensations he was creating in her rolled through every inch of her body, taking her completely over.

"Oh God," she whimpered. "So good."

Her words seemed to excite him even more, and the oral pleasure he was giving her intensified. When he sucked on her clit, she could no longer hold back.

"Yes. God. Yes." The time without him was over, and she drowned him in her drops of pleasure.

He licked up every drop, holding her legs over his shoulders.

"I need you in me, Nic," she said, trembling. "Please."

He looked up from between her legs and smiled. She could see her cream glistening on his lips.

"And I want to be inside you, sweetheart." He stood and reached into the pocket of his jeans, pulling out a condom.

He rolled the rubber down his thick shaft, and then got back on top of her. She loved the feel of his body on hers. She heard him moan as he slipped his cock into her pussy. As he stretched her insides, electricity spread throughout her body, sending her into overdrive.

He thrust into her again and again. She clawed at his back, wrapping her legs around him. It felt so good to be with him again, enjoying the pleasure he gave her. Her body's movements synced with his. Her pussy ached and her clit throbbed. Each time he sent his cock into her, she got nearer to the edge. She was mad with desire. She needed release.

"I'm close," she panted out. "So close."

"I'm close, too." His thrust became more powerful, more fierce. She could see the primal hunger reflected in his eyes as he drove deeper and deeper into her.

All at once the pressure inside her burst and she climaxed violently. Every part of her shook and she felt her pussy contracting around his cock.

He let out a hot groan before sending his cock into her depths in one final thrust. "Fuck. Yes, baby. So good."

He collapsed on top of her, and she loved feeling his muscled frame covering her body. She could feel her heart beating wildly inside her. She placed her hand on his chest and could feel his heart pounding ferociously, too.

"Nic, I've missed this so much."

His eyes narrowed. "You're mine, Ashley. All mine. No one else's. Forever."

She felt like the wind had been knocked out of her. "No one else's? You still don't get it, do you, Nic?" She could feel the tears well up in her eyes. "I was so certain after tonight's date that you finally understood. But now I know you don't."

"Ashley, I love you." The confusion she'd witnessed from him when they'd broken up had returned to his face. "Don't you love me?"

"You know I do, but you also know I love Sylas. I think you've known that since we saw each other last in Chicago."

"I can't share you, Ashley." Nic's tone was deep with emotion. He seemed to be choosing his words carefully. "How does a man share the woman of his dreams with another man, even if that man happens to be his best friend?"

"It's because of love, Nic. You love Sylas, even though you've been angry. And I know he loves you, too."

"So? That doesn't change a thing, Ashley."

"You love me. I love you. I love Sylas. That's what is important. Love. The question isn't how does a man share the woman of his dreams with another, but how much does he love her? Do you love me enough to share me with Sylas?"

Nic stared at her for what seemed like forever. Finally, he stood and said, "Ashley, I don't understand any of this."

The tears streamed down her cheeks. She took his hand and looked up at him. "Then let me help you understand. Please, Nic."

He shook his head and began dressing. "What you're asking doesn't make any sense to me. I should be enough for you. I don't understand this town. I don't understand how Phoebe could be married to three men. And I definitely don't understand why you want me to share you with Sylas." He looked her straight in the eyes. "I should go."

"Please, Nic. We can work this out."

"I could never share you." He walked to her front door and opened it. "Good-bye, sweetheart."

He left, closing the door behind him.

Sobbing, she felt her heart breaking apart again.

Chapter Nine

Nic stared at his reflection in the mirror. His eyes were red. No wonder. He hadn't slept since leaving Ashley.

"Fuck." He pounded his fists on the sink's counter. Once again, he was getting the short end of the stick. Typical. That's how his entire life seemed to always go. He loved her. *That should be enough.* But it wasn't. How could it be? What did he have to offer her?

His father's liquor-soaked breath spoke to him from the past. *"You're a worthless piece of shit, boy. No one wants you. Not me. Not your whore mom. No one."*

"Fuck you," Nic said aloud, but the old demons he'd fought back were haunting him again. He got his wallet and pulled out the photo of Pop Jim and Mama Gayle. Unlike his biological parents, Jim and Gayle had loved him. They were his foster parents for two years and had even started the paperwork to adopt him. God, he missed them.

"What should I do?"

The two loving people just smiled back at him from the photo.

Ashley deserved to be happy. If he couldn't give it to her and Sylas could...

I know what I must do. But knowing it didn't make it any easier. This was going to be the hardest thing he'd ever have to face, and he'd faced the devil in the eyes and lived to tell about it.

* * * *

Sylas sat across from Patrick and Sam O'Leary in Blue's Diner. Desirae had just left after bringing them coffee and taking their orders.

"So, Sylas, how did the date go last night?" Patrick asked.

"It appeared to go extremely well. We were all laughing, enjoying the food. The conversation was great. And to all appearances, Nic seemed to be enjoying himself. But I know him too well. It was all a façade."

Sam sat down his cup. "Are you sure?"

"Oh yes, I'm sure. When we got back to the hotel, we walked in together. Not a word was spoken. Not even a good night. Complete, total change. I don't believe Ashley knew Nic was putting on a front."

"Why do you suppose he was acting like that?" Sam said.

"You remember me telling you about how he grew up in foster care?"

"Yes."

"It goes deeper than that, I'm afraid. Nic's parents were no good. His dad was sent to the pen for life when Nic was only five years old. Homicide."

"Damn," Patrick said. "That poor guy."

"Nic's mother was a drug addict and didn't give a damn about him. Child Protective Services took him away from her and placed him in foster care, which ended up not being much better. His first foster parents were alcoholics and abused him."

Sam and Patrick didn't say a word but he could see on their faces the rage at the idea of anyone harming an innocent child. The O'Leary brothers were good men.

"Nic's second home was filled with warmth and love. Unfortunately, that couple died in a car crash on the way to pick him up from school. Nic still carries a picture of them in his wallet. After he lost them, Nic shut everyone out."

"How old was he when that accident happened?" Patrick asked.

"He just turned nine. The only thing he found solace in after they died was his studies, which he excelled at. Nic didn't act out, but no one could reach him. Because of that he was moved from foster home to foster home, in the hopes that one might be able to connect with him." Sylas took a sip of coffee as his mind traveled back to when he first met Nic. "He enrolled in my high school the middle of our sophomore year. Nic kept to himself and had no friends. We bumped into each other at the public library in the section where the law books were shelved. We struck up a conversation and found we both had the same dream of becoming a lawyer. His foster dad who had died in the car crash had been a lawyer, and my mom worked as a court reporter, which had got me interested in the law. We became very close. And the rest is history."

"I can understand where your friend, your brother, is coming from now," Sam said.

As if on cue, Nic walked into the diner.

"He's here," Sylas told them, "and heading this way."

"Hi, Sylas." Nic was visibly upset, though he was holding it in fairly well.

"Nic, this is Patrick and Sam O'Leary."

They shook hands.

"Sorry to interrupt," Nic said.

"No problem," Patrick said. "Looks like you two have something important to discuss."

Sam stood. "Patrick and I need to warm up our coffee anyway. So we'll give you some privacy."

He and Patrick excused themselves, taking their coffee cups and moving to the diner's long counter.

"Sit down, Nic. What's up?"

Nic took the seat across from him. "I came to congratulate you."

"For what?"

"For winning." Nic's face darkened.

Sylas saw sadness in his eyes. Nic looked like he'd lost twelve rounds in the boxing ring. "What the hell are you talking about, Nic?"

"I'm talking about Ashley, Sylas. What else? It's over. You win, Sylas. She's all yours."

"All mine? You still don't get it, do you? She made it clear back in Chicago what she wanted, and I believe what she still wants and needs." Sylas could see that he was about to lose his friend again, but this time it would be forever if he didn't do, say something that would turn Nic around. He leaned forward. "That's both of us, Nic. Can't you see that?"

"You sound just like her."

"Nic, what do you mean by that?"

"I went to her apartment last night, after our date."

"You what?"

"You heard me. I knocked on her door offering to help her with her studies for the bar exam. But I had other things in mind that I wanted to happen. I thought if we made love again that I could once and for all get you out of her mind. But it didn't work."

Anger welled up inside him. "What the hell is wrong with you?"

"Everything, apparently."

Hearing the anguish in Nic's voice crushed him. "Listen, buddy. I want you to talk with Patrick and Sam. They're helping me to get a better grasp on how the Destiny way of life can work. They're brothers and they've been married to the same wonderful woman for over fifty years. If you love her, Nic, you need to be willing to learn about this life at the very least."

"I do love her, but I can't do this, Sylas."

With a heavy heart, he watched Nic walk out of the diner.

Patrick and Sam came back and sat down.

"Didn't look like it went well," Sam said.

"It didn't." He told them what Nic had said. "I thought if he could just talk to you two he would come around. But I'm afraid he's going to turn down the job here and go back to Chicago."

"It's time for an intervention." Sam turned to his brother. "What do you think, Patrick?"

"I couldn't agree more. That young man needs to hear what you and I have to say."

"But not just us," Sam said. "I've got some other men in town in mind that can help Nic see what kind of future he and Sylas can have with Ashley. Matt and Sean aren't biological brothers and look how happy they are with Jena."

"Are you going to ambush him?" Sylas asked, wondering exactly what Sam and Patrick were planning.

"Not in so many words, but yes," Sam said. "It'll be good. I promise."

Desirae brought their meal. "More coffee, fellas?"

"Please, and the check," Patrick said. "We're in a bit of a hurry."

"Coming right up." She left their table.

They wolfed down the delicious breakfast and then headed to Phase Four.

Zac Gold met them at the door. "Welcome, Sylas."

They shook hands. "Mr. Gold, nice to meet you."

"Please. Just call me Zac. I understand that you want to take a look at our club. I'm happy to give you a tour. If you have any questions, feel free to ask." Zac led them into the building. "This is the reception area. Members must sign in before entering the play areas of the club."

Play areas? "I'm sure we have some clubs like this in Chicago, but I've never been to one before. I don't know that much about it."

"Then you need to come to our next munch."

"What's a munch?"

"That's where members meet up at a local restaurant with people like yourself who are interested in learning more about the life."

"I have a lot to learn," he confessed. But if Ashley was into this kind of kink, then he was more than willing to try to get a grasp on it.

"So did I and every other Dom at one time," Zac said. "We were all newbies. Let me show you the main room."

The tour impressed Sylas. Phase Four wasn't seedy at all, which was what he'd been expecting. The main room had stages. He wondered what it would be like to have Ashley on display for all eyes to see.

Zac showed him a selection of sex toys—paddles, floggers, dildos, and violet wands, the latter of which was used to deliver electric shocks to submissives.

"Women actually like being shocked?"

"Some do and some don't, Sylas," Zac told him. "You have to get to know your sub and her desires. Our club is all about pleasing the submissive."

"I've learned a lot today, but I'm at the very beginning."

"Yes, you are," Sam said. "Zac, like I said on the phone earlier, Sylas needs a crash course."

"I have the training room all set up." Zac looked at him. "Sylas, if you have the time, we can begin today. After today, you can make the decision if you want to become a Dom or not."

"I'm here to learn, so yes." For Ashley, he would do anything. "Lead the way, Zac."

Chapter Ten

Ashley wore her sunglasses into her workplace. Her eyes were bloodshot from crying all night.

Phoebe came out of her office. "I thought I told you to stay home and study today, Ash. What are you doing here?"

"I need to talk to you," she said, and the tears started falling.

"Oh my God, Ash. What's wrong?"

"Nic," was all she was able to get out.

Phoebe rushed to her side and put her arm around her. "Let's go into the break room. I want to get you a cup of coffee, and we can talk this out."

She sat at the table and Phoebe poured them each a cup. The coffee did help to calm her nerves and help her gain her composure a little. She told Phoebe everything that had happened with Nic and Sylas and how Nic had showed up after the date.

"He left, Phoebe. It's over. It's completely over."

"This is all my fault, Ash." Phoebe's tone was filled with guilt and regret. "I was sure that if Nic and Sylas saw you again and got a taste of Destiny, they would come around. I'm so sorry, but I can tell how in love they both are with you. Why do men have to be so stubborn?" Phoebe's cell rang. "It's Jason. Give me a sec."

"Sure." She wiped her eyes.

"Hi, honey, this isn't a good time. Ash and I are having a heart to heart about her guys. Oh really? Tonight?" Phoebe smiled and winked at her.

Jason must have said something that made Phoebe happy. Who wouldn't be happy in her situation? Phoebe was expecting twins and had three men who adored her. It hadn't always been that way for her friend. It had taken years for the Wolfe brothers to come around. But they had come around.

In her heart, Ashley had held onto the hope that Nic and Sylas would do the same with her. But now she knew that was never going to happen. It was next to impossible. Nic had made it clear that he would never be willing to share her.

"That's a great idea," Phoebe told Jason. "I'll keep Ash company while you guys are at the intervention. I love you, too. Bye."

"Phoebe, you don't have to stay with me today. I'll be okay."

"Yes, you will. Better than you can imagine."

She was puzzled. "What do you mean by that? What did Jason say to you?"

Phoebe told her about the intervention that Sam had set up for Nic. It was scheduled tonight at his hotel room. Nic had no idea that it was going to happen.

She wasn't surprised about Sam arranging the meeting. People from Destiny always had each other's best interest at heart. They were doing this for her. They wanted her to be happy. That was the same reason that Phoebe had lured Nic and Sylas to town in the first place. "What about Sylas?"

"He'll be there, too. Sylas is on board, Ash. Totally. Your man is at Phase Four right now getting his first Dom lesson. Can you believe it?"

"That really surprises me. I'm so happy he's willing to give us a chance. I think Sylas does understand, but I just am not sure Nic ever will."

"Honey, you can't know that. This is all new for him and Sylas. It's a lot to deal with at one time. Trust me, I know my guys need to mull over anything they aren't quite familiar with. For instance, when I told them I was pregnant with twins, they were very excited but they were also very apprehensive. Just like any man. I'm sure Nic and Sylas are no different. Once they get the full picture of what it's actually like living our lifestyle, I have no doubt they will be completely on board and enthusiastic. This intervention will work to show them what kind of future they can have with you. They will make the right decision. You'll see."

She wished it were true, but she'd been down this road before. Back in Chicago. "Nic said that he can't share me no matter what. He's done mulling it over. He's made up his mind to end it with me. I'm not sure that anything or anyone will turn him around. I told you about his childhood, didn't I?"

"You did. He had such a hard life."

"Maybe I'm asking too much from him."

Phoebe shook her head. "He told you he loves you. That's what you said. Do you believe him?"

"Yes. I know he does, and I love him. Like all the songs say. You have to be willing to let your true love go."

"That's bullshit. Those songs should be banned. I almost lost my three wonderful men because I bought into that belief. Let me tell you something, Ash, and listen good—if you love him, you hold on with both hands as tight as you can. You do whatever it takes to help him see what kind of future that he, Sylas, and you can have." The passion in Phoebe's voice couldn't be missed. "You know better than anyone that Nic needs a family, Ash."

"Yes, I do. I wish Sylas and I could be his family."

They heard the bell that alerted someone had walked into the reception area.

"That's got to be Jena," Phoebe said.

"Another secret meeting that I didn't schedule?"

"Not a secret. I just set it up this morning, Ash."

Wondering what the appointment with Jena was about, she stood. "I'll go get her and take her to the conference room."

"You most certainly won't." Phoebe left her seat. "You're off the clock today. Remember?"

She followed her into the reception area. "What clock? There's never been a clock here. Hi, Jena."

Jena was always prepared, and as usual, she had her computer bag with her. "How are you?"

"She needs to be studying," Phoebe said, "but I'm actually glad she's here. I want her in on this meeting."

This wasn't the first time that Phoebe had sought out Jena for her incredible skills. Jena was one of the top cyber intelligence experts in the country and was unsurpassed in her ability to uncover hidden information. What case did Phoebe want to engage her for?

Once in the conference room and seated, Jena asked, "How can I help you, Phoebe?"

"Ashley and I are working on a case for Jennifer Steele. And at present our position is very weak. There's a good possibility we might lose." Phoebe explained to Jena about the alleged claim on Jennifer's ranch. "Ashley has had doubts that the man is actually Bill's brother. The more I thought about it the more I began to believe she might be right. That's why we need your help, Jena."

"I'd be happy to help." Jena pulled out her laptop and placed it on the table. "Anything for Jennifer. She's a wonderful woman and a friend. Jennifer and my mom have become very close. And Kimmie just adores her. I can start right now."

"That's fantastic," Ashley said, standing. "I'll get you copies of everything we have on the man claiming to be Walter Steele." She left the conference room and went to her desk. It was good to be working because it kept her mind off of Nic and Sylas. But she knew she would have to face them head on.

She turned on her computer. As it booted up, she wondered what Sylas thought about Phase Four. Was he still there? And what about Nic? What was he doing right now? What would he think about the intervention the men of Destiny had planned for him?

So much for keeping my mind off of them.

She signed into her computer and brought up the files on Walter Steele. She'd made hard copies for her and Phoebe already. Besides Jena needing copies, with Nic and Sylas coming on board, they would need them, too. She hit the print button.

Her mind wouldn't let go of her troubles, despite all her efforts. How the hell was she going to pass the bar next week? *One foot in front of the other, Ashley. That's the only way.*

As she was placing the pages into folders for Jena, Nic, and Sylas, something caught her attention on the property tax record. It looked different.

Last week, she'd printed out the information from the Florida county appraisal district the man lived in. Normally, Phoebe had her go over all the records for their cases, but with her bar exam coming up, Phoebe had decided to do the reviews herself. That had created a backlog.

Ashley pulled out the original file she'd printed on this case. She placed the property tax record next to the same record she'd printed today.

There was a significant difference.

Today's copy had Walter Steele's middle initial on his property tax records for 2013 as an *L*. That matched the Swanson County birth certificate of Bill's brother. Walter Leon Steele. But the page she'd printed last week had a *D*. She read the timestamps on both pages. Identical. *Not possible.* The records were different.

She clicked on the intercom to the conference room. "Phoebe, can you and Jena come out here? There's something I need to show you that I believe Jena can help with."

When they were at her desk, she showed them what she'd found. "It doesn't make any sense. I'm the one who saved the file. They should be identical. How is this possible?"

"Someone with incredible technical savvy can forge all kinds of records and timestamps." Jena motioned to the keyboard. "Do you mind if I give it a try on your computer?"

She stood. "Please. You're the expert."

Jena sat and started typing feverishly. Things started popping up on the screen that looked strange and unfamiliar. It was clear that Jena was reaching deep into the core code of the machine.

"No one else has access to your computer but you and Phoebe?" Jena asked, never slowing down her fingers.

"That's right," Ashley said, but then she recalled what had happened yesterday with Anna. "I don't know if this means anything, but an urgent call came in from Walter Steele's attorney yesterday. I had to leave my desk because Phoebe was on another call. When I came back, Anna was sitting in my chair in front of my computer."

"Anna, who works at TBK?" Jena asked. "Anna Banks?"

"Yes. She lives in my apartment complex. We started going on runs together a month ago."

Phoebe's eyes narrowed. "A month ago was when Jennifer got served with papers from Walter Steele's attorneys."

"Yes. In fact, as I recall it was the very next day she invited me to run with her. That can't be a coincidence, can it?"

"It's not," Jena said, pointing to the screen. "See this coding? I've run across it before. It's Kip Lunceford's work. Anna infected your computer. Someone has been able to access it remotely since yesterday, and I have a good idea that someone is Kip's sister, Cindy Trollinger. Ashley, thank God you saw this when you did. Any later, and the fallout would've been horrible."

Phoebe brought out her phone. "I'll call Jason and tell him what we've discovered thanks to Ash. If Anna is in town, he can bring her in for questioning."

Jena also held her cell out. "I've got to let Matt and Sean know immediately so that we can cut off her access to TBK. If Anna is working for Trollinger, I have no doubt she's re-infected TBK's network with Lunceford's viruses."

As Phoebe and Jena filled in their husbands about what they'd discovered, Ashley wondered how long Anna had been working with Trollinger.

"Thanks, honey. Please keep us in the loop." Phoebe ended her call. "Jason is going to Anna's apartment now and will call Easton Black on the way."

"Jason is sending Nicole and Jaris to TBK to see if she might be there." Nicole and Jaris were Jason's deputies.

Jena clicked off her phone. "Anna has been working from home all this week."

"I guess we know why now," Phoebe said. "I'll call Jason back and let him know they don't need to go to TBK."

"Actually, I think it's good that Nicole and Jaris are headed to our offices. Matt and Sean might be able to help figure out where Anna might be if she isn't at her home. Plus, we don't know if Anna was working alone or if there were others at TBK helping her. The moment we hung up, Matt was going to call the Knights to fill them in."

"I wonder what this has to do with Jennifer's case." Phoebe tapped her fingers on the desktop, something she always did when she was trying to figure out a difficult issue. "There has to be a connection. Why else would someone change Walter Steele's middle initial?"

"I agree," Ashley said. "This man must be an imposter. Once we research the change in his initial, I'm betting we'll have proof. My guess is that Trollinger wants to get a foothold close to Destiny. If she could get title to the Steele Ranch, which is valued at over twenty-eight million, through the man claiming to be Walter Steele, then Trollinger could work through him to keep up her attacks on our town. Her M.O. is always to use others to get her dirty work done. Anna is just her latest patsy. You know what happened with your sister-in-law and the Reverend Willie. "

"If it hadn't been for Josh and Jacob, we would've lost Carrie for good." Jena sighed and looked at the screen. "Shit." Jena started typing feverishly on Ashley's keyboard.

"What's the matter?" she asked.

"Whoever has remote access to your computer has been watching and listening to us through your computer's microphone and camera."

Shit was right.

Chapter Eleven

Having finished his crash course at Phase Four, Sylas couldn't wait to talk with Ashley. "Thanks, Zac. I really don't know how I'll ever repay you."

"No need, buddy. Great job for your first lesson. I find you to be a natural. Embrace your Dom side. Go find Ashley. Let her know how you feel. Be happy."

"I will." Sylas left the club, knowing that this lifestyle—the one Ashley desired—was what he wanted, too. Zac had told him that there would be many more lessons in the future, but today had been a very good start.

He brought out his cell and sent Ashley a text. *I need to talk to you. Can we meet?*

Everything Zac had showed him spoke to something deep inside. Being a Dom wasn't about abuse. It wasn't only about control, although that was definitely a part of it. Being a Dom, as Zac had showed him, was primarily about trust. The submissive gave her trust after the Dom earned it. The relationship between a Dom and his sub was a thing of beauty and mystery, something sacred between them alone. Just like the safe word given to the sub, every part of the lifestyle had a reason and a deep meaning.

He intended to be the Dom Ashley wanted him to be. He would have to learn even more about her than he already knew so that he would be able to give her the pleasure she needed the most.

His phone buzzed. He looked at Ashley's response to his text. *I need to talk to you, too. Can you meet me at my apartment in ten minutes?*

Yes, sweetheart.

He got in his rental car and drove north on West Street. Passing the Dream Hotel, he turned left on McDavish. He was glad that Ashley had suggested her apartment instead of the hotel. He didn't want to accidentally run into Nic in the lobby before the big ambush. He wasn't certain how Nic would respond to the O'Learys' intervention plan, but he had no doubt that Nic would respond positively to Zac's instruction about what it meant to be a Dom. Sylas knew Nic better than anyone. The BDSM lifestyle was tailor-made for Nic.

He pulled up to the call box next to the complex's driveway gate. He punched in Ashley's apartment number.

"Hello?"

"It's me, sweetheart."

"Okay, I'll buzz you in. Park in the visitor space next to the office. I'll meet you there."

He heard three beeps and the gate opened. When he cut the engine, he saw Ashley walking his direction. He jumped out of the car and pulled her in tight.

She wrapped her arms around him.

He gazed into her deep blue eyes. "Hi, sweetheart."

"Hi." She led him to her apartment, which reflected her personality in so many ways. Warm colors and soft fabrics filled the space.

Without hesitation, he put his arms around her and pressed his mouth to hers. "I've been waiting a long time to taste your lips again, Ashley." Before she could respond, he gave her another kiss, and another, and another. "God, I've missed you."

"I've missed you, too." Her face was beautifully flushed. "Why don't we sit?"

He nodded.

She sat down and he moved next to her.

"I like your place, sweetheart."

She smiled. "I can't believe you went to Phase Four."

"Man, this is a small town." He grinned. "How did you find out?"

"Phoebe told me."

"I'm not sure how she knew, but you are right. Destiny is a small town."

Ashley laughed. "There are no secrets here."

"That's why I wanted to talk to you. To tell you about my visit to the club." He touched her cheek. "You're everything to me, sweetheart. I love you. That's why I came to Destiny. I wanted to learn everything about the life you wanted, so I went to the club you belong to."

"Who told you I was a member of Phase Four?" She looked a little nervous, which made her even more desirable to him.

"The O'Learys. My appointment with them was to ask questions. They certainly gave me some answers. They were the ones who introduced me to Zac."

"The O'Learys, was it? I'm not surprised." She giggled. "Seems that you're fitting into this small town quite well."

"Easy to do with the people who live here. I've never been anywhere quite like it. I've learned so much in such a short time." He stroked her hair. "I want what you want, sweetheart. I get it. All of it. I was blind back in Chicago. A fool. We belong together."

"We? You and me? What about Nic?" Doubt appeared on her face.

"When I say 'we,' I mean you, me—and Nic. He's my brother, and he loves you, too."

"I know he does, but it's over. He told me so." She told him about what had happened between her and Nic last night.

"It may seems hopeless, Ashley, but Sam and Patrick have planned an intervention for him."

"I know about that, too. I'm not even sure that will be enough to turn Nic around." She leaned her head into his chest. "Do you think I should join the men when they meet with Nic?"

"I would love for you to be there, but this is an intervention by the men of Destiny for Nic. He needs to hear what they have to say, sweetheart. The only person who knows Nic as well as I do is you, Ashley. I never saw him open up to anyone like he did when you were dating. I'm sure he told you about his childhood. That's why he has so many issues."

"I agree. I have no idea how he was able to survive such hell. No wonder he's pushing me away. I can understand why. I ran away from both of you trying to protect my heart. It didn't work. It only made things worse."

"Sweetheart, I know Nic, and I know you. You think he's pushing you away to protect himself. It's the other way around. I'm sure that Nic believes he's protecting you by ending it." He told her about what Nic had said to him in the diner. "He called me the winner and left before I could convince him to stay."

"You might be right, Sylas. Maybe he believes he is somehow protecting me. But he also is taking care of himself. He has trust issues because he has lost so much his whole life."

"Trust. That's where you and I come in. We will assure him until he is confident that we aren't leaving. No matter what. That the three of us belong together. We are family."

"I hope he can see that," she said.

"He will. Trust me. Nic may not feel like it right now, but he is still my brother." Sylas thought about what Sam had told him earlier. "Always will be."

"If you have faith in him staying, then I have faith, too."

"That's my girl." He leaned in and kissed her deeply. His balls grew heavy and his cock hardened. "Now, sub, we are going to your bedroom where I can show you some things I learned today at Phase Four."

Her face brightened. "Yes, Sir."

He stood, trying to remember everything Zac had taught him. *Commanding tone. Confidence. Clear instructions.* "Where's your bedroom, sub?"

"Down that hall, Sir."

He loved hearing her call him "Sir." It heated his blood. "Follow me." Taking his first step to her bedroom, his foot caught on the leg of her coffee table and he landed on his ass.

Her hands flew to her mouth and she burst out laughing. "I'm sorry, Sir. I can't help myself."

He started laughing with her, reaching up and pulling her on top of him. "Zac said I needed more lessons, and I guess he was right."

"You're doing great, Master." She kissed him. "It means the world to me that you want to learn."

"Maybe we just make love how I know best right now, throwing in a few things I learned at the club. I promise, with more training, I'll be the Dom of your dreams, baby."

"You've always been a great lover, Master." She smiled. "But maybe today you could use my help getting to the bedroom."

"You're a sassy sub, aren't you?"

"Wait. I thought we were going vanilla."

"Vanilla? Zac said that meant conventional sex. Right?"

She nodded.

He lifted her in his arms as he got to his feet. "Is that what sex with me was like back in Chicago?"

"No. Never. You may just be learning about the life, but you have tricks up your sleeves that would make most Doms green with envy."

"Like what?"

Her cheeks turned red. "That thing you do with your tongue."

"Oh, really?" He carried her into the bedroom. "Would you like me to do that trick with you now?"

"More than anything."

"Good." He could see that she was getting turned on and that made him want her all the more. He lowered her feet to the floor.

"You want my wicked tongue. Then earn it, sub." He sat down on the bed. "Give me a show."

Ashley's face lit up. She grabbed her cell. "I have the perfect song for you, Master."

Suddenly a tune with a heavy bass beat filled the room.

She sat her phone down and began moving her body to the sensual song. Seeing her hips sway so seductively made him rock hard. *Damn, I shouldn't have asked for this. I'm not sure I can hold myself back.*

Slowly, she unbuttoned her blouse to the rhythm of the music. When she tossed it to the floor, he leaned forward, wanting more. She removed her bra, exposing her gorgeous, full breasts. She smiled and once again gyrated to the music.

Concentrate, Sylas. Be a Dom. Be the Dom she needs. "Tell me what you want me to do to you, sub."

"I want you to touch me."

"Touch you where? Be specific." He was getting into his role. He loved how she responded to his words.

"My breasts, Sir. I want you to touch my breasts."

"Show me. Use your hands. Pretend they're mine."

She nodded and moved her delicate fingers over her mounds.

"Pinch your nipples, sub." He took off his shirt. He couldn't hold back much longer. He wanted her. Wanted her more than anything. Two months had gone by since he'd seen her naked. But a Dom was supposed to put his sub's needs before his own, and Ashley seemed to need him to take things slow, to raise her desire to a state of deliriousness. To do that for her he must keep his self-control. With that in mind, he willed himself to stay put on the bed despite the hunger for her inside him. "Pinch them hard."

She obeyed, closing her eyes and moaning.

"Do you just want me to touch your breasts, sub? Or do you want me to touch you other places, too?"

She opened her eyes and their gazes locked. "Other places, Master. Please." Her breathy words poured gasoline on his internal fire.

"Take off the rest of your clothes and show me," he commanded.

"Yes, Sir." She took off her shoes, slipped out of her slacks, and stepped out of her thong. As the song she selected continued playing, Ashley ran her hands over her gorgeous naked body, writhing to the music.

He stripped out of the rest of his clothes and stood. Dom or not, he couldn't wait any longer. He lifted her into his arms and lowered her onto the bed.

He moved on the mattress next to her and started massaging her breasts. "God, you feel so good."

She licked her lips. "So do your hands."

He pinched her nipples lightly, and she moaned. He bent down and kissed them, circling his tongue around her buds. She arched her back off the mattress, clearly wanting more. Her scent of desire made him crazy and hungry for her body.

He ran his hands down her sides. She felt warm, soft, perfect. Moving down her body with his mouth, he tasted her smooth skin. So sweet. So delicious. He had to have more. He positioned his head between her thighs and lifted her legs over his shoulders.

"God, your pussy is beautiful."

She laughed. "No pussy is beautiful, Sylas. Not even mine."

"Sylas? What happened to Master?"

"I'm sorry, Master."

"How would you know if your pussy is beautiful or not, sub? You're not a Dom. I am."

He felt her tremble and looked in her eyes.

"Yes, you are a Dom, Master." She was excited by his dominance, and that pleased him. "You're my Dom. My Master. I'm your sub."

"Yes, you are." He ran his tongue over her wet pussy, loving the taste of her sweet cream. He licked her folds, taking in every drop on them.

"Oh, God. That feels so good, Master. Please. Don't stop."

He had no plans on stopping. He wanted her to come so he could drink down her orgasm.

She pushed his head down tight onto her pussy. "More. Please. More."

He sucked on her clit, and she gasped.

He continued bathing her pussy and drinking her juices.

"Oh. Oh. Oh. Master. I'm coming."

Liquid poured out of her pussy and he drank it all. He could feel her writhing, and he knew he was pleasing her.

His cock was throbbing and his balls were aching. He was mad with want, want for her, want to be inside the woman of his dreams.

"Please, Master. I need you in me. Please."

Impossible to hold back any longer, he grabbed the condom out of his jeans and put it on. He got on top of her, sending his cock into her sweet, tight pussy.

"Oh my God. You feel so good."

He kissed her trembling lips. "This is where you belong, sub. With me."

"Yes, Master. With you."

He pushed into her, loving the feel of her pussy tightening around his cock. In and out. Holding her tight, he kissed her neck, continuing to thrust into her. She clawed his back. The frenzy between them was hotter than it had ever been before. Now that he had her back in his arms, he was never going to let her go.

His entire body stiffened and then he came with a groan.

He held her close, kissing her tenderly. Their bodies remained entwined together as their heartbeats and breaths began to slow.

He gazed into her blue eyes. Being with her again felt like heaven. She was his future. "I love you, Ashley."

"I love you, too." She kissed him. "You will be my Dom forever."

She dozed off in his arms. After hearing what had happened with her and Nic last night, he had no doubt she hadn't slept much. She looked so peaceful. He knew there was only one way to ensure her happiness. Nic had to let his walls down and realize that the three of them belonged together. The only hope he had was the intervention. He prayed it would knock some sense into Nic.

Sylas left the bed, careful not to wake Ashley.

Chapter Twelve

Ashley awoke to her doorbell ringing. She reached for Sylas, but he was gone. Making love with him again had been amazing. Where was he? Her head was still foggy.

The doorbell rang again.

She glanced at her alarm clock on the nightstand. 7:11pm. *Sylas is at Nic's intervention.* She'd slept over two hours. She got out of the bed.

Once again, the doorbell rang.

"Coming," she yelled, grabbing her robe. "Hold on."

She peered through her peephole and saw Phoebe. She remembered Phoebe had said she was coming over.

She opened the door.

"I see you got some much-needed sleep, Ash." Phoebe walked in, carrying a couple of bags. "I brought dinner from Phong's Wok— sesame chicken, crispy beef, sweet and sour shrimp, egg rolls, crab puffs, and fried rice."

"I have the perfect wine to go with this meal, but that sounds like a lot of food for just the two of us." She grinned, glancing down at Phoebe's belly. "It's the four of us, isn't it? Oh no. You can't have wine."

"Don't remind me, Ash. But you can, and I will enjoy watching you drink it. This may sound strange, but do you have chocolate milk? It's just one of the crazy cravings I've been having. I just can't get enough chocolate."

"I don't have chocolate milk." She looked in her refrigerator. "I do have some chocolate syrup to mix with the milk."

Phoebe smiled. "Could I just have the syrup?"

They laughed.

They sat down at the kitchen table and began enjoying their meal.

"I'm really glad you came over because I'm so nervous about Nic's intervention."

"Trust me, Ash. You know the men of Destiny. They'll be able to help Nic understand that this life will work for him, that being with you and Sylas will give him the perfect life. I just know it."

"Hopefully you're right. I love him so very much. And I love Sylas."

Phoebe's eyebrows rose. "Ashley Vaughn, you're glowing. Did you see Sylas after you left the office?"

She grinned. "Yes."

Phoebe leaned forward. "Well?"

"He came over and we talked."

"I can tell you did much more than talk." Phoebe never settled for vague answers, just one of the reasons she was such a great attorney.

"I'll tell you this much. His first time as a Dom was absolutely fabulous. Not trying to change the subject, but what is going on with Anna?"

"Very subtle, Ash. You definitely are trying to change the subject, but here's what I know so far. Jason went to her apartment. Ethel gave him a search warrant. Anna wasn't there. She wasn't at TBK either. No one has seen her."

"Since Trollinger had access to my computer when me, you, and Jena were talking at the office, I'm sure she tipped Anna off about what we'd discovered. I bet Anna has left Colorado."

"Jason put an APB out on her. I don't think she can get far."

* * * *

Talking with his travel agent on his cell, Nic continued his trek around the park in the center of Destiny. He'd hoped the walk might clear his head and help him put things in perspective. It hadn't. "Anything?"

"All the seats are taken. Let me check another airline," the agent said.

He had been trying to get an earlier flight back to Chicago all day without any luck. After leaving Ashley the way he had, all he wanted to do was be as far away from Destiny as possible. *How the hell am I going to live without her?* He wasn't sure but knew it was best for Ashley that he left. For Ashley and Sylas. They could get on with their lives with him out of the picture.

"I'm sorry, Mr. Walker, but there is nothing available."

"Damn." His ticket was for a seat on the last flight tomorrow night.

"Sometimes seats open up at the last minute. When will you be at the Denver airport?"

"It's a four and a half hour drive from here. I will be leaving shortly." He should have left hours ago, but hadn't been able to bring himself to go. His bag was packed, sitting on his hotel bed. What had held him back? He knew once he left Destiny there would be no chance of ever seeing Ashley again.

"The earliest flights after midnight aren't until five in the morning, Mr. Walker. Would you like me to arrange a hotel for you near the airport?"

"That won't be necessary. Just get me on one of those morning flights."

"Yes, sir. I'll do my best."

He clicked off his phone and looked up at the dragon statue ahead. It reminded him of the books Pop Jim and Mama Gayle had given him his first Christmas in their house. Definitely happier times then. But those days were long gone.

Tolkien's incredible dragons and mighty heroes in *The Hobbit* had delighted Nic when he was a boy. Despite the struggles and hardship, the good guys in his books always won in the end. But now Nic knew that wasn't always the case.

"No more stalling. It's best I get out of here." He walked directly to the hotel.

When he entered the lobby, the man at the front desk waved him over.

"Yes?"

"I have a message for you, Mr. Walker." The young man behind the counter nodded. "You are supposed to go to the Rocky Mountain Room. It's down that hall, the last door on the left."

"Do you know why?"

"No, sir, I don't. I just started my shift."

As he walked down the hall, Nic wondered who might be waiting for him in the Rocky Mountain Room. The only people he knew in Destiny were Ashley, Phoebe, and Phoebe's husbands.

Once he opened the door, Jason, one of Phoebe's husbands, greeted him. Behind Jason were several men sitting at a conference table. He spotted Sylas first.

"Hi, Nic." Jason was in his uniform, with a gun holstered to his belt.

"Hey, Jason." He recognized Mitchell and Lucas, Phoebe's other husbands, who he'd also met at the rental house. Phoebe's plan had been for him and Sylas to share the place. *Share?* That seemed to be the main word for Destiny's citizens. Living with Sylas wasn't going to happen.

It was a good thing he hadn't given notice to Braxton, since he had no intention of taking the job with Phoebe.

The only other men he recognized at the table were the O'Learys, Patrick and Sam, who had been with Sylas at the diner this morning.

Jason led him to a seat at the long conference table.

"What's this about, Jason?"

"First, let me introduce you to everyone."

"I know you and your brothers. And I've already met the O'Learys."

"This is Matt Dixon and Sean MacCabe, who work at TBK. And this is Eric and Scott Knight, who own TBK."

"It's very nice meeting each of you, but I still am wondering what this is all about."

Sam rose from his chair. "Nic, I am the one who organized this meeting. As you probably know, we had an appointment with Sylas. He had come to us with many concerns about Destiny's lifestyle."

Nic stood. "I don't mean to interrupt, but I'm planning on leaving here."

"Hold on, Nic," Sylas said. "Please, just hear us out."

"I guess since Sam has gone to all this trouble, I don't want to be an ass." He sat back down.

"Thank you, Nic," Sam said. "I appreciate it. As I was saying, when Sylas came to us his biggest concern was you. I understand that you two are like brothers."

"We were, once."

"Just like I told Sylas. Once brothers, always brothers. Sylas cares very deeply for you. And if I'm not mistaken, you care very deeply for Sylas. Brothers can disagree, but they don't lose their love and respect for each other."

"Thank you, Sam. But this isn't going to change what I'm going to do. I am leaving as soon as this meeting is over. It's for the best."

"The best for who, Nic?"

"For Sylas and Ashley, of course."

"Can you really say what's best for Sylas and Ashley? My understanding is that they want to make a life together with you."

"I don't mean to be disrespectful, sir, but I could never share a woman with anyone. Brother or no brother."

"Which brings me to the main reason I set up this meeting. Sylas has told me how you feel. All of these men in this room would like to tell you how happy their lives are—sharing one woman. All I ask is that you hear them out. If you still want to go after that, no one will try to stop you."

Nic still couldn't understand how families like these men had worked, how it was even possible. Curious to find out, he said, "Fine. That's fair enough."

Sam turned to Patrick. "Since you're the oldest here, you're up first, brother."

"Sam, do you always have to bring up my age?"

All the men laughed.

Patrick grinned. "I'm not that much older than he is, Nic. But with age does come some wisdom. Sam, it's your story to tell, too."

"But you tell it so much better."

Patrick grinned and then turned to Nic. " When Sam was sixteen and I was seventeen, we immigrated to the United States. We had no reason to stay in Ireland. Our father had died in World War II and our mother had passed away with a broken heart a year later. We needed a new beginning."

"I can relate," Nic said, thinking about Pop Jim and Mama Gayle. "My parents died when I was young."

"So you understand why we wanted new surroundings, a whole new place to start over."

Nic nodded.

"Sam and I settled in Springfield, Missouri. We went to work for the local newspaper." Patrick brought out his pipe, and though he didn't light it, brought it up to his lips. It was obvious this man was a wonderful storyteller. "On our very first day at the paper we saw the most beautiful girl we'd ever laid eyes on. She was the editor's daughter, Ethel Mae Young. She had deep blue eyes, like the sparkling Irish Sea, and long blonde hair, like golden flax. I knew immediately that I wanted to get to know her better, despite our difference in class. Sam felt the same way, and told me so. At first, we thought going after the same girl would be a lark. One of us would end up with her. The other would step aside. That had been the plan. Or so we thought.

"But Sam and I fell hard for our sweet Ethel. We both wanted her. Like you and Sylas, we each dated her separately. She was the light of our life. As the weeks turned to months, my brother and I began to resent each other. I felt like the time Sam spent with her was time I should be with her. He felt the same way. On Sam's twentieth birthday, he told me that he was going to ask Ethel to marry him. I informed him that I had already bought her a ring and was going to propose as well. Sam smugly told me, 'May the best man win.' I was so arrogant at that age that I laughed. 'I am the best man and I will win.' At that point, we knew what we had to do. We had to ask her together. Then the loser would know the truth and back away.

"We hadn't realized that Ethel wanted both of us, but we each learned she did when we popped the question. You should have seen Sam and me. There we were on our knees before the love of our life demanding she choose between us. With tears streaming down her face, she refused. 'I can't choose. It's an impossible choice. Please. You're breaking my heart. I love you both. That may be wrong, but it's true. I can't see either of you anymore. It's just too hard.' The three of us were devastated. Ethel ran upstairs to her bedroom. Sam and I left and went to a pub. We were heartbroken. We didn't know what to do. After several pints and letting go of the jealousy that had torn us apart, we came to the same conclusion. It wasn't fair to ask her to choose. The very next morning we joined the army.

"After basic, we were sent to Korea, where the war had broken out. I was captured by the enemy. The entire time I was their prisoner—seven long months—the only two people I could think about were Ethel and Sam. That's when I met my first dragon."

"Dragon?" Nic smiled.

"Stay on track, brother. That story is for another time."

"True. I still had no clue how Sam and I could work things out with Ethel. I woke up in a military hospital, next to Colonel Franklin McDavish. Sam was there, too, and came to visit me every day.

"McDavish had taken a bullet and had a high fever. He rambled on and on about needing to get back to his brother and their wife. He was constantly saying 'their wife.' I believed his words were brought on by his fever but it did get me to wondering what it might be like if Sam and I could marry Ethel together. I didn't believe it was possible, but I couldn't stop thinking about it, especially with McDavish next to me. When Frank's fever broke, I asked him about what he'd said. At first, he held back. You have to realize that was 1952, Nic. But when I told him about our story—mine, Sam, and Ethel's—he brightened up and told me about his hometown, Destiny, Colorado.

"When Sam arrived that night, I told him that everything Frank had been saying during his fever was true. Frank and Sam shook hands. We asked so many questions. Every answer Frank gave filled us with hope.

"Once I was back on my feet, Sam and I returned to Missouri to find Ethel, the woman of our dreams. Having heard about my capture, she greeted us with tears."

Sam snorted. "She was crying for me, too, brother. You might mention I took a couple of bullets in Korea."

Patrick laughed. "Anyway, Nic. Ethel was happy to see us both alive. When we told her about what we'd learned from Frank, she was elated. Sam and I had bought a ring for her together. Once again, we knelt in front of her, but that time, unlike before, we didn't ask her to choose between us. She said 'yes,' and the rest is history. We've been happily married ever since."

"Thanks, Patrick," Sam said, turning back to Nic. "So you see, son, if it hadn't been for Frank, God rest his soul, my brother and I wouldn't have the wonderful life we have with our beautiful bride. That's why I set up this meeting for you. I wanted to give you the same chance to hear what life can be like here that Patrick and I heard from Frank."

Nic stood and clapped. The other men joined him. His cell rang. He looked at the screen. It was his travel agent. "Excuse me, fellas. I need to take this."

He stepped out into the hallway. The agent told him about a seat that opened up on an earlier flight, but he declined. No way was he leaving early. He needed to hear everything these men had to say. "I'm still in Destiny. I've decided to take the original flight I was booked on. Thank you for your help."

When he returned to the Rocky Mountain Room, he said, "Thank you for sharing your story with me, but Sylas and I aren't related. We may call each other brother but we don't share the same blood."

"Which brings us to our next speakers, Nic." Sam smiled. "Matt Dixon and Sean MacCabe."

Matt spoke first. "Our wife, Jena, and Ashley are good friends."

He and Sean told the story about how they'd met and fallen in love with Jena. "So you see, we're not blood brothers either, Nic. But in every other way we are."

The rest of the men told Nic their stories until late in the night.

At the very end, Sylas stood. "Nic, you're my brother. Even though we had a bump in the road, you've never stopped being my brother. I know you love Ashley, and you know I love her, too. Just like Patrick and Sam, we just didn't know what to do about it. Now we do. Sam's intervention was about you, but hearing all these men's stories also helped me. This is new for us, but I believe that you and I can make Ashley happy. You only had a loving family for a short time. This is our chance for the three of us to be a family for the rest of our lives. I love you, bro. So what do you say?"

Wracked with emotion, Nic stood and walked up to Sylas. He pulled him in for a hug. "I'm sorry, bro. For everything. I do love you. And you're right—I do love her." He turned to the other men in the room. "Thank you, but I still don't understand how the sex works. I assume you are all heterosexuals."

They all laughed.

"You assume right," Patrick said, smiling.

"Not that we have anything against gays or bisexuals," Sam added. "In fact, we have gay families and bisexual families in Destiny. This town respects everyone's right to love any way that they want."

"You should see our gay pride parade, Nic," Mitchell chimed in. "It's over the top and everyone participates—gay, straight, whatever."

Nic couldn't get over how accepting these men were. "So...do you take turns?"

Sam laughed. "Now you sound just like Sylas. That was exactly what he asked us. I'll give you the same answer that my wife gave him. Sometimes it's separate. Sometimes it's together. Take it from me, a man who's been married for over five decades. Sexuality is a journey that is discovered day by day."

"And night by night," Patrick teased. "You can teach old dogs new tricks, Nic. The fun is learning with the woman you love."

Imagining what making love to Ashley for the rest of his life would be like, Nic smiled. "Sylas, you and I need to talk to Ashley."

"Yes, we do." Sylas looked him in the eyes. "So you're convinced? You want this? You believe that you and I can make it work with Ashley?"

Nic laughed. "Now who sounds like they need convincing? Yes. I do. I love her. You love her. She loves us. She wants us both. I know it's late, but I have to see her. I've put her through hell. I can't go another second without letting her know how much she means to me and that I want us to be a family. Are you with me, Sylas?"

"For the rest of my life, bro."

Chapter Thirteen

Sitting in her comfy PJs and slippers, Ashley stared at the page of the law book in her lap. She'd read the same sentence at least a dozen times. She just couldn't concentrate, even though she needed to be studying. Phoebe had left at eleven-thirty, which was over an hour ago.

Surely the intervention is over by now. Why haven't I heard anything?

She decided to put on a fresh pot of coffee. She was thankful for the little bit of sleep she'd gotten after making love to Sylas. But there would be no more sleep tonight. She was too wound up.

Please let Nic see that we belong together. This can work. He has to believe it.

Sylas had made it clear to her that he wanted the three of them to be a family. That's all she wanted, too. She'd dreamed about it back in Chicago. Was Phoebe right? Was everything going to turn out right?

Her doorbell rang, startling her. She dropped the can of coffee, spilling the dark grounds on the floor.

A knock followed.

"Ashley, it's me. Nic. Sylas is here, too. We need to talk."

She ran to the door and flung it open. "Oh my God, you're together. Please tell me that the intervention worked."

Nic swept her up in his arms and swung her around. "I'm so sorry, baby. Please forgive me. I realize now that I let my past get in the way of our future. I've told you what my parents were like. But what I didn't tell you was what it felt like to be in that position as such a young child. I spent years listening to my father tell me how no one wanted me, not even my mother. He told me I wasn't good enough to love."

Ashley's heart broke for Nic. "I'm so sorry you had to go through all that. But you have to know it's not true. You are one of the most lovable people I've ever met."

"I know in my head that he was an awful person and that his words aren't true, but when you told me you wanted both of us, I felt like I wasn't good enough to have you alone. All those feelings from my childhood came rushing back."

"If your father wasn't serving life in prison, I'd hunt him down and make him pay for what he did to you," Sylas said.

"Thank you, brother. It means so much to me that you feel that way. Ashley, I love you so much. I've been a stubborn-ass fool and any other adjectives or slurs you want to fill in that you believe are appropriate."

When he placed her back on her feet, she looked in his eyes. "No adjectives, Nic. Just three words. I love you." She glanced at Sylas. "And I love you." Looking back at Nic, she asked, "Is that okay with you?"

"It's more than okay with me." He pressed his mouth to hers, causing butterflies to flutter inside her.

"If your father's words start playing in your head again, just tell us. We'll do anything to help you," Ashley said.

"That's right. We can plot out all the bad things we want to do to the asshole. That should make you feel better." Sylas laughed.

She saw Nic smile, and that told her that he had completely turned around. There was no jealousy in his eyes. He understood everything she wanted and was okay with it.

Nic turned to Sylas. "He loves you as much as I do, sweetheart. And we're brothers. That never changed even when I denied it. I have so much to learn. I hope you can be patient with me."

"With me, too," Sylas added, kissing her.

"The three of us together can work through anything," she said. "I'm just so happy I can hardly stand it. This is the best day of my life. I will remember it forever."

They each kissed her, proving beyond a shadow of a doubt that the intervention had worked its magic.

"We need to toast this," she said. "I've got a bottle of Chardonnay in the refrigerator we can open. And if you're hungry, there's leftover Chinese."

"Both sound good to me," Sylas said.

"Same here," Nic chimed in. "Lead the way, baby."

When they got to the kitchen, she saw the mess she'd made. "I forgot about this. Give me a second to clean it up."

Nic shook his head. "You sit, sweetheart. Sylas and I can take care of this. Where's your broom?"

She pointed to the utility closet and sat down.

"I'll get the wine." Sylas opened her fridge and retrieved the bottle. "Where's your opener, honey?"

"I'll get it."

"No," he said firmly.

Nic returned and started sweeping up the grounds.

"Am I supposed to sit here like a princess?"

"Yes," they said in unison.

She smiled. "The opener is in that drawer. The glasses are in that upper cabinet to the left of the sink. This is so much fun, watching you two, but I have to admit I'm not use to being waited on."

Nic emptied the grounds into her trashcan. "You better start getting used to it because that is what we intend to do from here on."

"Well, do I ever get a turn?"

Sylas placed a glass of wine in front of her. "Only if you're sneaky enough, sweetheart."

She smiled. "So that's how it's going to be."

"Yes. This is how it's going to be from now on." He bent down and kissed her.

She felt tingly all over.

Nic put the broom away and took a glass from Sylas. "After all that work, I need one of those kisses, too." He pressed his mouth to hers, making her toes curl.

She looked at her two wonderful men. "I think we would be more comfortable on the sofa in the living room for our toast."

Nic held out his hand for her, holding his glass in the other. With her glass in her left hand, she took his with her right. Sylas held his glass and the bottle and they all walked to the sofa.

"Before we sit, I think we should each give a toast." Nic held up his glass. "I'll go first. Here's to my brother and the girl of my dreams. Forever a family."

They clinked their glasses together and sampled the wine. It tasted sweet.

"I'll go next," she said. "This is the happiest day of my life because of my two great men. Here's to many more happy days."

They clinked their glasses and drank again.

"Sylas, our girl needs her glass refilled and so do you and I."

"On it, bro." Sylas poured more wine. "My turn. I never dreamed we could be so happy together." A teasing grin appeared on his face. "And here's to our future children."

Ashley lifted her glass and then pulled it back. "Children?"

Sylas and Nic looked at each other and then turned back to her. "Yes," they answered together.

"Okay, then."

Another clink and they emptied their glasses one more time.

"Guys, two full glasses of wine in a few minutes." She felt wonderfully warm all over. "I need to sit down, and no more wine for me. A buzz is fine, but I don't want to pass out."

"And we don't want you to pass out either, sweetheart." Nic ran his hand down her arm. "This is our first night together as a family. The toasts were nice, but they are only the beginning of this celebration."

"Amen, brother." Sylas leaned back and put his arm around her.

"Let's get more comfortable." Nic kicked off his shoes. "That's better."

Sylas did the same. "Yes, it is." He touched her on the cheek. "My lips are so cold, baby. I need them warmed up." Sylas moved in for a kiss.

Surrendering to his mouth, she wrapped her arms around him as he traced her lips with his tongue. She could feel Nic's hand on her thigh. *He's watching Sylas kiss me.* Knowing that made her so excited.

When Sylas released her, she said, "Are they warm now? Mine are."

Smiling, he ran his finger over her lower lip. "Yes, they are."

Nic nuzzled her neck. "My lips are so lonely, baby. I need them to touch yours."

He devoured her mouth, and Sylas stroked her hair. Her dream of being with them together was coming true and their kisses and caresses ignited a blaze inside her. She was burning up, getting hotter and hotter.

Nic leaned back.

She gazed into his sexy eyes. "Is your mouth lonely now? Mine isn't."

"Neither is mine," he answered.

She touched each of their faces. "My lips feel so good. They are just right."

"And we want to keep them that way." Sylas kissed her neck.

"That's sounds like a good plan to me," Nic added, and began nuzzling her neck from the other side.

"That feels so good." *Nic and Sylas don't seem uncomfortable with this at all. I wonder what they are feeling inside.*

When they each reached for her breasts at the same time, their hands bumped.

"Oops." Nic smiled. "We still have a lot to learn, don't we?"

"But what fun it will be," Sylas said.

"I've got an idea," Nic said in his familiar teasing tone. "Her left breast is mine for tonight. You have dibs on her right."

Sylas grinned. "I love that idea."

She laughed. "And what happens when you go lower? How do you plan on dividing me up then?"

"Can we just take this one step at a time? Ashley, this is my first ménage," Nic said.

"Mine, too," Sylas added.

"Same for me," she said.

"I'm glad to hear that," Nic said. "And I bet so is Sylas."

"I certainly am."

"It's true, guys. We're all newbies when it comes to threeways, but I love the way this is starting out."

Nic smiled. "Shall we practice some more?"

Once again, Sylas said, "Amen, brother."

It took her two men no time at all to synchronize their caresses. No more accidental bumps between them. All their focus was on her, and that was thrilling.

The pressure began to build inside her as they slowly stripped her out of her clothes. She loved being naked between them, their hands moving up and down her body, their lips kissing her mouth, neck, and nipples.

She sent her fingers between their legs and felt their hard cocks bulging through the denim of their jeans. She unzipped them, one at a time, pulling out their long, thick dicks.

"That feels good." Nic licked her throbbing nipple. "Stroke us, sweetheart. This is what you've wanted. And Sylas and I only want to make you happy."

"You really would make me happy if you would strip out of your clothes."

Nic leapt from the sofa. "God, you are so beautiful. Your wish is my command, sweetheart." He started unbuttoning his shirt and then stopped. "Wait. Sylas told me on the way over more about what this lifestyle we all are entering is about."

"He did?"

"Yes, I did." Sylas stood and moved next to Nic.

Seeing them standing next to each other with their jeans unzipped and their cocks bulging was so enticing.

Nic winked at her, and that melted her insides. "I haven't taken the crash course from Mr. Gold that he has, but I get the idea of what you really need from us." Nic's tone deepened. "Stand up, sub." He turned to Sylas. "It is 'sub,' right? That's what you said in the car."

"Absolutely right." Sylas's eyes remained on her, which pleased her. "Keep going, Nic. You are doing great."

"Remove my shirt, sub."

She got on her feet. "Yes, Master."

"I like being called that by her."

"Me, too, Nic. Me, too."

She stepped in front of Nic and finished unbuttoning his shirt. She pulled it off of him and placed it carefully on the coffee table.

"You want to touch my chest?"

"Yes, Sir."

"Knock yourself out, baby."

She ran her hands over his muscled pecs and down to his six-pack.

"Now, sub. Take off Sylas's shirt." Nic's rising hunger could be heard in every syllable he spoke.

This is really happening. My dream has come true.

She could feel her pussy start to ache and the wetness between her legs begin to pool. Sylas was wearing a T-shirt, so she pulled it off of him and placed it next to Nic's on the coffee table.

"Now my jeans, sub. Then Sylas's. Do it." His eyes had a primal look to them that made her tremble.

"Yes, Master." She got on her knees in front of him and pulled his Levi's down to his ankles.

Nic stepped out of his jeans. His hard cock stretched out of the waistband of his white briefs.

She thought about pulling down his underwear before moving to Sylas, but didn't. His instructions had been clear. His jeans, then Sylas's. She scooted over in front of Sylas. He cupped her chin. "You enjoying this, sub?"

She gazed up into his blue eyes. "I am, Master. Very much."

He smiled. "Finish what Master Nic told you to do."

She pulled his jeans down and he stepped out of them.

Sylas wore boxers, and like Nic's briefs, they weren't able to contain his hard cock either.

"How am I doing at this Dom thing, Sylas?" Nic asked.

"I'm certainly no expert, but in my opinion, you're doing just great. What do you want our sub to do next?"

"I want to feel her delicious mouth on my cock."

Sylas grinned. "You've got her, Nic. She licked her lips when you said that."

"I did?" She felt heat rush to her cheeks.

"Yes, you did, sub." Sylas touched her shoulder. "And it made me want you even more."

She hadn't even been aware that she'd done that.

"God, she is beautiful, Sylas. Those lush lips. I want them on me."

She wrapped her hand around his cock and squeezed.

He groaned.

Grabbing his balls with her other hand, she repeated his words back to him. "Your wish is my command, Master."

She ran her tongue up and down his shaft and then, circling the head where a tiny liquid pearl sat, she drank it down.

"Fuck, you two look so hot." Sylas's words were heavy with desire. "I can't wait for those lips to be on me."

"You heard your Master, sub." Nic tugged on her hair, which caused more moisture to pool between her thighs. "Suck him. Suck Sylas."

The jealousy between them was no more, and she couldn't be happier. Keeping one hand on Nic, she grabbed Sylas with her other hand and began licking his cock.

He groaned. "Damn, that feels incredible. You better stop, sub. I don't want to come yet."

"Yes, Master." Tasting their pre-cum on her tongue drove her wild.

Nic knelt down next to her and smiled. "Look at her pouty lips, Sylas. She wants more."

"Let's take our sub to the bedroom," Sylas said. "We can show her a whole lot more there."

Nic nodded and helped her to her feet. Sylas lifted her into his arms and they took her into the bedroom, lowering her to the mattress.

Nic and Sylas got on the bed next to her and started kissing and caressing her into an incredible state of delirium. Their foreplay was turning into a free-for-all. Nic and Sylas seemed insatiable, each taking a turn licking her pussy while the other swallowed her breasts.

"I want you both now. Inside me." She was crazed with desire for them and fisted the sheets, as her body seemed to have a mind of its own. "Please, Masters. Please."

Sylas stopped licking her pussy and started fingering her ass. "Do you have lubricant, sweetheart?"

"No, Sir." Disappointment rolled through her.

Nic kissed her. "Not to worry, baby. Do you have olive oil?"

"Yes." Her heart was racing wildly.

"That should work just fine. Where is it in your kitchen?"

"The pantry on the second shelf."

Nic leapt from the bed. "Keep our girl's engine running, Sylas. I'll be right back."

"My pleasure." Sylas sucked on her clit, causing her to gasp.

Nic returned with the bottle of olive oil and got back in the bed. "I can't wait to get inside our sub's pretty ass."

Sylas released her clit and looked up from her pussy. "Damn, I forgot to get my condom out of my jeans. Your turn, Nic. I'll be right back." He jumped out of the bed and rushed into the other room.

"Roll over, baby."

She obeyed, and he began applying lube to her ass.

Sylas returned. "Got it."

Nic laughed, and she felt his thick fingers stretching her anus. "Next time, you and I need to be better organized."

"I agree, Nic. But look at how turned on she is. Not too bad for our first ménage. Are we doing okay, honey?"

"Better than okay," she panted out. "Just hurry. I need you both so bad. Please."

"Yes, baby. We will. Nic, you go first. I'll finger her pussy while you take that gorgeous ass nice and slow. Once you're all the way inside her, roll her on top of you so that I can send my cock into her sweet pussy."

After hearing Sylas's words, she trembled. This was a first for her—two men taking her simultaneously. *My men. They're taking me, claiming me. My Doms.*

Nic climbed on top of her. She could feel the tip of his dick pressing against her anus. Sylas reached under her and sent one of his fingers into her pussy while pressing on her clit with his thumb.

Nic held her wrists and slowly pushed his cock all the way inside her ass. The sting that came from the stretch subsided quickly, replaced by a blazing need for more. As Sylas had set up, Nic rolled onto his back, pulling her with him so that his cock never left her body.

She looked up at Sylas. He moved on top of her, rubbing the side of his shaft against her swollen, wet folds. "How bad do you want this, sub?"

"More than anything, Master. Please. I need you in my body. You and Nic."

"Then your wish is our command, sweetheart." He thrust his cock into her pussy in one long stroke.

She gasped and clawed Sylas's back. The two men she loved with all her heart were inside her. She'd dreamed of this moment a hundred times, but never imagined it would be so overwhelming and intense.

"You okay?" they asked her in unison, their bodies completely still, their cocks throbbing inside her.

"Oh God, yes. Yes, Masters." The pressure continued building, driving her mad. "More. Please. More."

They began thrusting into her, but their rhythm was off.

"Shit, Nic. We're out of sync," Sylas said with a grin. "She deserves better than this, even if it is our first time."

She laughed. "It all feels great to me, Master. Please, don't stop."

"Sylas. To the beat. One." Nic thrust into her and Sylas did the same a half-second latter.

A moan slipped out of her. "Yes."

"Two." Their thrusts came closer together.

By the time Nic got to "four," he and Sylas had matched their tempo perfectly.

"Oh my God. Oh my God. Oh my God." She couldn't stop repeating those words. She'd never felt anything like the kind of sensations they were bringing out inside her. She writhed between them like a live wire as she got closer and closer to the orgasm she so desperately needed. Every single nerve in her body was electrified, vibrating hot and violent.

She couldn't contain herself. "So good. So good. So good."

"Fuck, yes, this is good, baby." Nic continued pushing in and out of her ass. "This is unbelievable."

"This is fucking off-the-charts incredible." Sylas deepened his thrusts into her pussy.

No longer able to hold back, she yelled, "I'm coming. I'm coming. I'm coming." The juices poured out of her like a river as she climaxed like crazy.

Nic grabbed her hips and drove his cock deep into her. "I'm coming, baby. Fuuuck."

"I'm coming, too," Sylas moaned. The final note of their synchronized symphony ended in melodic bliss.

Chapter Fourteen

As rays of the morning sun came through the window, Sylas slipped out of Ashley's bed. She and Nic were still asleep. Quietly, he walked out of the room and shut the door behind him. He grabbed his clothes off of the coffee table, where Ashley had placed them last night. *What a night. God, the best ever.*

He walked into the kitchen and opened the pantry, pulling out the can of coffee. He started a pot. Thankfully, Ashley hadn't spilled all the grounds. She'd looked so cute in her PJs and slippers, sitting in the kitchen chair while Nic swept up and he got the wine ready.

Sylas was truly happy. He loved her so very much.

Opening the refrigerator door, he saw everything he needed to cook for their breakfast—a dozen eggs and a package of bacon. And he'd seen a loaf of bread in the pantry, so they could have toast, too.

Toast? He grinned recalling how much fun they'd had clinking their glasses together, celebrating their new family.

He almost laughed out loud when he went to the pantry. *I'm glad I don't need the olive oil. It's still in the bedroom.* Although he wouldn't have minded oiling her up some more. Now that was the kind of breakfast he could sink his teeth into.

When the bacon finished cooking and he started scrambling the eggs, Nic came out of the bedroom. He closed the door and gathered up his clothes, dressing quickly.

"She still asleep?" Sylas asked him.

"She's out. I believe she could sleep a couple of more hours." Nic stepped next to him. "Smells delicious, bro. Anything I can do to help?"

"Set the table and put out butter and whatever jams she has."

"On it." Nic went to work. "You know, Sylas, if I had known it could be this good back in Chicago, I would have never acted the way I did."

"Me, too. I was an ass to her. But never again. She's going to come first in our lives from now on."

Nic put his hand on his shoulder. "Hell, Sylas. I just love this life. We are a family. For real."

"For real and forever."

"I want you to introduce me to Mr. Gold as soon as we get back from Chicago. I want to learn everything about what it's going to take to turn me into a Dom."

"When I took the crash course, I realized that I'd only scratched the surface. Gold told me that a Dom never stops learning." The eggs were finished and he emptied them into a bowl by the platter of bacon and toast. He brought them to the table. "It's a lifelong pursuit. I signed up for some classes next month. You and I can go together."

"Damn right. Ashley deserves our best. I hate that we have to be away from her for three weeks, but we've got to give notice and wrap things up back home."

"True, but it's not our home any more. Destiny is. I hate it, too, but Ashley needs to focus on her bar exam. Because of us, she didn't crack a book last night. It's probably good that we won't be around to distract her."

"Distract me?" Ashley walked into the kitchen. She was wearing a white terry cloth robe that he would love nothing more than to rip off of her. "Distract me from what?"

"From your studies for the bar, sweetheart." He pulled her in close and kissed her lightly on the mouth. "I made coffee. Would you also like orange juice with breakfast?"

"Yes, please," she said. "I like being distracted by you guys." She smiled. "You know the bar exam is offered more than one time a year."

Nic shook his head and hugged her, also kissing her good morning. "Not a chance. You're taking it next week as planned. Phoebe is depending on you."

"I know. I just am so happy that we're together. I'm not ready to dive back into my studies yet."

"I understand, sweetheart. So it's a good thing that Sylas and I are both flying out tonight, which will allow you to get back to work on passing the bar."

She frowned. "I don't want you to go."

Sylas poured them coffee and juice. "Sweetheart, it's only for three weeks." *That does sound like a lifetime to be away from her.* He looked at Nic and could tell he felt the same way. But they needed to encourage her, so they were both trying to sound positive.

"Didn't you say you're both on the same flight and that it leaves out of Denver at four-thirty today?" she asked, sitting at the table.

"That's right, baby," Nic said. "We'll need to be on the road no later than eleven, and that will be cutting it close. It's a four and a half hour drive and we'll both need time to return our rental cars and get through airport security and to our gate."

"That's only two hours from now," she said.

He grabbed her hand. "Two hours that we can enjoy together. I could use your help at the hotel packing my bags."

Nic laughed. "Makes me wish I hadn't packed mine already. Here's an idea. Let's finish breakfast and the three of us take a shower together. That'll save us time and will be fun, too."

Ashley nodded, wolfing down a piece of toast. "All done." She leapt from her chair. "Last one in the shower has to clean the dishes." She dropped her robe to the floor and ran to the bathroom.

He and Nic died laughing.

"Shall we?" Nic asked.

"For the rest of lives." They ran after the woman of their dreams.

* * * *

Standing in front of the Dream Hotel, Ashley couldn't bring herself to stop holding onto Nic and Sylas. Tears streamed down her face. "My happiest day is turning into my saddest day."

"It'll be okay, honey," Nic said. "We will call, Skype, text, e-mail, write, smoke signals…"

Sylas added, "Hell, we'll send carrier pigeons if need be."

She grinned and wiped her eyes. They always did know how to make her feel better.

"I know this is going to seem like a long time, baby." Nic kissed her, and she melted into him. When he released her lips, he stared at her with his sexy eyes. "But we have the rest of our lives where we won't have to be apart."

"I know."

"I love you, baby."

"I love you, too."

Nic got into his rental car.

She turned to Sylas. "I just wish I could go with you and Nic to Chicago. I could help pack up your apartments for you."

Sylas pulled her into his arms. "You have your exam and Phoebe needs you here." He pressed his mouth to hers, and on her tiptoes she wrapped her arms around his neck. "I love you, sweetheart."

"I love you, too."

"Nic and I will call you tonight." He got into his rental car.

She watched her two wonderful men drive away. She wiped her eyes. "It's only three weeks, Ashley. You will survive."

* * * *

With a pistol and silencer in her lap, Anna Banks sat in the run-down shack Cindy Trollinger had sent her to when all hell broke loose on their plan. Ashley had blown Anna's cover.

Ashley, the fucking bitch, is to blame for all my problems.

Now she was stuck in this horrible place waiting for the burner phone to ring. Trollinger had given the cell as well as the gun and silencer to her the day they had made their agreement. It had sounded like easy money to her. All she had to do was break into the law firm's computer network to give Trollinger remote access and enter a few lines of code into TBK's systems. The law firm was a piece of cake. She warmed up to Ashley and waited for the right opportunity to enter the virus. TBK was a little more challenging, but she was successful. If TBK lucked out and realized something was wrong, even their best, Jena, would have a difficult time isolating Trollinger's code.

It had sounded so good at first. *I was going to be a fucking millionaire, but now I'm nothing but a goddamn felon.*

"Fuck. What's taking Trollinger so long? She better do something soon. I'm not going to stay here much longer." *Great, Anna. Now you're talking to yourself like a crazy person.*

She looked at the cell's screen. "Ring, damn it."

Chapter Fifteen

Ashley touched the images of Nic and Sylas on the screen of her laptop. "I miss you both so much. It's hell being apart."

"We miss you, too," Sylas said.

Nic nodded. "If it wasn't for Skype, I think I would go crazy."

"Why don't you forget about your notice at Braxton and head to Destiny in the morning?" she asked them. "I just need you so much."

Nic shook his head, which didn't surprise her. He and Sylas were honorable men and would give their boss the appropriate time to transition their work at Braxton. "Only two weeks to go, baby. I know it's hard, but you have to be patient."

She was surprised that he was being so sensible. She would expect that from Sylas, but not Nic. He was the more impulsive of the two of them. At least most of the time.

"It's more than two weeks, Nic. You and Sylas don't get back to Colorado until a week from next Thursday. Right now it's 5:45pm Friday night Mountain Time, which means it's an hour later where you are. So that's two weeks and five days and two hours until your plane lands and I see you again." She grinned. "Not that I'm counting."

Nic looked at his cell. "And ten minutes. I'm counting, too, baby."

"And thirty-two seconds," Sylas added, and they laughed. "We're anxious to be back together. But like Nic said, we need to be patient."

Nic nodded. "I'm glad Phoebe gave you the day off so that you could meet us at the airport."

"Phoebe is the best. She's almost as anxious as I am for you two to get back to Destiny. She's scrambling with the Steele Ranch case.

Jena hasn't been able to prove that Walter Steele is an imposter yet but is still working on it. I offered to come into the office yesterday, but Phoebe told me emphatically not to."

"Of course she did," Nic said. "She wants you focused on studying."

"I'm nervous but I'll be glad when I finish the exam Wednesday. Even if I don't pass this time, I will be ready for a break."

"You'll definitely pass," Sylas said. "Now, let's get back to it. Nic, you want to quiz her next or you want me to?"

"Wait a second." She looked at the time on her screen. "You both said we could take a ten minute break. I have two more minutes left...Masters." She paused and stared at their images on the screen. "There is so much in my head right now that if someone asked me what a deposition was I'd probably say it had something to do with a train stop."

They laughed.

"Baby, you're going to do great," Nic said. He turned to Sylas. "But I believe our girl is right."

"Me, too," Sylas said. "Ashley, close your books. Take a long break. Relax."

"I'm not sure I should, guys. I only have the rest of tonight, Saturday, and Sunday before I have to drive to Denver. I'll have some time Monday night in the hotel to study for the test the next day, but that's it. I'm a wreck. I just know I need more time."

"You're going to be fine, sweetheart," Nic said. "Your answers to all the practice questions we've gone over with you are spot on."

"B-but—"

"No more, sub," Sylas said in a deep, demanding tone. "Do as your Masters have said. Turn on your television, sit back, and really relax. At least for an hour. And only study until midnight. No more than that. Take a bath. Get in bed. And quit worrying that pretty little head of yours."

Hearing his command made her feel better. Her guys believed she was ready. *God, I hope I am.* "Yes, Sir."

He smiled. "I love you, sweetheart.

"I love you, too, but I miss you so much."

"You'll see us before you know it."

Nic turned to him and shook his head. "I love you, sweetheart. We'll Skype you in the morning."

She frowned. "In the morning? Why do we have to stop and end our Skype session now? You don't have to go to the office, do you? It's night time."

"As a matter of fact, baby, we are going into the office," Nic said. "Sylas and I have a bunch of work we need to finish for the morning."

"But that's Saturday. Attorneys aren't supposed to have to work on the weekend." But she knew better. Phoebe worked most weekends.

Nic smiled. "Just be patient, and we will talk to you tomorrow. Goodnight. I love you."

"I love you, too."

"I love you," Sylas said. "Sleep well, sweetheart."

"I love you. Bye."

* * * *

Nic closed his laptop and turned to Sylas. "You almost blew our secret."

Sylas looked surprised. "How?"

"When you said to her, 'You'll see us before you know it.' But lucky for you I changed the subject before she could ask what that meant." Nic placed his laptop in his bag and sat it by his suitcase. "If she wasn't worried about her exam I bet she would have caught on. Our girl is very smart. What time do we need to leave?"

"The O'Learys' jet will be landing at the airport shortly. We've got a little time yet."

Sylas had become quite close to Ethel and her husbands. So had he. But both of them had been shocked and thrilled when the O'Learys had offered their corporate jet so that they could return to Destiny to spend some time with Ashley.

"I can't believe that we will be at her door in less than five hours, bro."

Sylas finished packing his bag. "I'm glad we're doing this."

"Me, too. Ashley is a nervous wreck. I think with us there she'll settle down."

"That's what Ethel said when she called and offered the plane." Sylas zipped up his bag.

He folded the sofa sleeper, which had been his bed last night, and placed the cushions back on the seats. His own apartment was already packed up. The movers were arriving to load Sylas's stuff on their last day at Braxton. Sylas had suggested that instead of moving to a hotel he should stay here until the move. Made sense, since they were going to end up at the same place, Phoebe's rental house.

"How about a beer before we head out?" Sylas asked him. "We've got a few minutes before the cab arrives."

"Sounds good to me."

"I wasn't surprised when Mr. Jenkins agreed to us taking the three days off next week to be with Ashley while she takes her exam." Sylas handed him a beer, holding one of his own. "He's really been good to us, Nic."

"He sure has. We can work remotely while Ashley is taking her exam, and I told Mr. Jenkins he could reach us by phone if anything came up." Nic drank the beer. "I can't wait to see our girl, Sylas. God, I know it's only been a few days but I miss the hell out of her."

"Me, too."

"But tonight we not only get to see her, but we also get to hold her again."

Sylas smiled. "I know what you're thinking, Nic, because I'm thinking it to."

"She needs to relax." Nic held up his beer. "Right?"

"I completely agree." Sylas clinked their bottles together. "To the woman of our dreams."

"Here. Here."

* * * *

The burner phone rang, startling Anna. "Friday fucking night, Trollinger."

"Calm down, Ms. Banks."

"Calm down?" Rage rolled through her. "You've got to be kidding. It's way fucking past time that you called me. I've been held up in this shack with nothing but fruit and beef jerky since Tuesday, not to mention I haven't had a shower. When in the hell are you going to send someone to get me the fuck out of here?"

"Do you want to be a millionaire or not, Ms. Banks?"

Anna was shocked to hear that. "I thought that chance was over for me when that bitch, Ashley, found out what I did to her computer."

"Only a small setback, so of course I've had to rearrange some things."

"What about the code that I put in at TBK? Has Jena discovered it?"

"I don't know yet. So far, our code is still working. And even though I no longer have remote access to the computers at the law office, I was able to get all of Phoebe's files for the Steele Ranch case before Jena shut our virus down."

"You mean we still might win?"

"Might? We will win, Ms. Banks."

Anna's mood lightened. Hope for her future was renewed. When she'd met with Trollinger last year, the woman had showed her a secret government report. How Trollinger had acquired it, she didn't know and hadn't asked. But the facts on the pages were clear. There was a fortune sitting beneath the Steele Ranch. Billions and billions of cubic feet of natural gas were just waiting to be pumped out of the ground.

Once the man posing as Walter Steele got title to the ranch, the money would start flowing. Anna's share was ten percent, which would give her the life of luxury she'd only dreamed of. She planned on moving to a house on the beach of a Caribbean island. It would be paradise all day, every day.

There was little doubt that Trollinger had more in mind than just making money from Steele Ranch. Anna was very aware of the havoc the woman had caused the town. But she didn't give a damn about Trollinger or Destiny. She only cared about the money. *Let her burn the town to the ground. Good riddance.*

"When can I expect your man to come get me, Cindy?" She was fairly certain that Trollinger hated being called by her first name, which was exactly why she did it. Very satisfying.

"Ms. Banks, Sheriff Wolfe put out an APB on you. It's too dangerous for you to leave. Every road in and out of Swanson County is being watched. You must stay put for a few more days."

Fresh fury exploded inside her. "No fucking way. You need to get me out of this hellhole, Trollinger, and you need to do it now."

"You want to blow your chances? Go ahead. Leave. I no longer need your services."

Anna wanted to scream. She wasn't about to lose the money for all she'd done for Trollinger. Right now, the woman had all the power. She had none. She had to trust her.

"I'm sorry, Ms. Trollinger. I'm just very frustrated. If Ashley Vaughn hadn't stuck her nose in where it didn't belong, none of this would be happening to me." *That bitch needs to pay.* "I don't have any more fruit and I'm out of bottled water. What can I do?"

"Just a minute."

She heard clicking coming through her cell. She guessed Trollinger was typing on her keyboard. Suddenly the line went dead.

"What? No." Had the call dropped? She stared at the burner phone, praying Trollinger would call back. Several minutes passed. The cell never rang again.

* * * *

Sylas stepped out of the O'Learys' corporate jet and onto the tarmac of Walden-Jackson County Airport.

The limo that the O'Learys had arranged for them was waiting by the plane.

Nic shook hands with the driver. "How long does it take to get to Destiny from here?"

"A little over an hour."

"Hear that, Sylas? If we're lucky, we will get to see our girl before the stroke of midnight."

"I can't wait, bro."

* * * *

Ashley stepped out of her robe and sunk into the warm water in her tub. Instantly, the tightness in her shoulders softened. She inhaled the lavender scent she'd added to the water.

She hadn't spoken to Nic or Sylas since their Skype session a few hours earlier. She'd been able to get in more studying without them. Of course, she preferred having the help of her incredible men.

Closing her eyes, she leaned back on the towel she'd folded up behind her head. She only wanted to think about Nic and Sylas and the future they had ahead of them. She needed to relax, but her mind just wouldn't settle down.

Phoebe was working the Steele Ranch case alone. The court date was approaching fast. She hoped that with Jena's help they would be able to prove that the man claiming to be Jennifer's late husband's brother was an imposter.

Ashley couldn't wait to have the bar exam behind her. She needed to be back in the office, taking the load off of Phoebe.

She was so excited for Phoebe and her husbands. They were going to make wonderful parents. Ashley had started a list of people she planned on inviting to Phoebe's surprise baby shower. *I will be taking Anna's name off that list.*

Nic and Sylas would also make great dads. Thoughts of having children with them made her smile. Her mind drifted back to the night the three of them spent together. God, it had been wonderful. She couldn't wait to have more nights with them, many more nights.

* * * *

As the driver drove the limo down the road, Nic looked out the window. "I can't see a thing, Sylas. I wonder how close we are now."

Sylas looked at his watch. "We've been on the road for fifteen minutes. Just over forty-five minutes until we see our girl."

"I feel like a little boy asking 'how much longer' every ten minutes. But I just can't help it."

Sylas laughed. "I've been checking my watch every five, so just keep asking."

"I will." Holding Ashley again in his arms was waiting for him at the end of this trip. It wasn't possible to contain his excitement. And he could tell Sylas was feeling the same. It had taken an intervention by some great men to get him to see what was best—best for him, for Sylas, and for Ashley. They belonged together.

He grinned and turned to his friend. "So how much longer, Sylas?"

* * * *

Anna slammed the burner phone on the table, breaking its screen. She didn't give a fuck. It was crystal clear that her partnership with

Trollinger was over. The woman had hung up on her and hadn't called back.

All Anna's plans were up in smoke and she had no place to go.

Next stop for me is prison. "Fuck. None of this would be happening to me if it weren't for that damn bitch, Ashley Vaughn."

She knew she had to get out of the state and locate a place she could hide. But the goddamn sheriff had put out an APB on her. Every cop in the state was looking for her car.

She needed another vehicle, and the only way she had left to get one was to steal. She snapped the silencer to the barrel of the gun. Her hands were shaking. She didn't have many options, and the ones she did have weren't good.

An image of Ashley appeared in her mind, and suddenly an idea occurred to her. That idea made her feel better and calm. "Why steal? Ashley won't be needing her car when I'm done with her."

* * * *

Sylas pulled Ashley's key out of his pocket for the umpteenth time since she'd given it to him. Nic also had a key. "One. Seven. Six. Four. One."

Nic laughed. "You're worse than I am."

"What do you mean?"

"You've been repeating Ashley's gate code over and over for the past five minutes. Are you afraid you'll forget it before we get to her complex?"

"Not a chance, buddy. I can't wait to see the look on her face when we knock on her door."

* * * *

Ashley slathered peanut butter onto her crackers and poured herself a glass of milk. This was one of her favorite nighttime snacks, a luxury she didn't indulge in very often. But she'd earned it. She'd studied hard. Nic and Sylas said she was ready, and she hoped they were right.

She sat down on her sofa and turned on the television. She needed something light to watch that would let her mind relax enough so that she would be able to fall asleep. The program she selected was a cooking competition show. The three chefs were baking desserts, which looked delicious to her. If she kept eating the way she had been the past few weeks, she would have to run two and three times a day.

She put down her glass, recalling the last run she'd been on. Her running partner had been Anna, who was still at large. She and Phoebe hoped that Anna would be apprehended soon. They believed once she was in custody they would be able to find out the truth of who Walter Steele really was.

* * * *

Looking in every direction, Anna rolled down her car window and entered the code at the security gate. She'd been able to get all the way to her apartment complex without being spotted.

She knew the only place that would be buzzing in Destiny this time of night was Phase Four, and she was nowhere near it. But she still needed to remain cautious and on guard. She had no intention of getting caught and being sent to prison.

She drove her car to the back of the parking lot. There was one empty space next to the complex's dumpsters. It was the best place to leave her car because the giant metal bins kept it from being seen from the street.

Wild Oaks was dark and silent. That was a good thing. She didn't want to be spotted by some nosy neighbor who would alert the sheriff's department. She'd thought about going to her own apartment to collect some personal things for her escape out of the state. But she'd tossed that idea aside, knowing she didn't have much time.

She was here for two reasons. One, to make that goddamn bitch pay. And two, to take her car. That was all. Nothing else.

* * * *

After placing her empty plate and glass in the dishwasher, Ashley stretched out on her sofa. She was getting sleepy but wanted to see if Chef Rosie's molten chocolate cake was going to beat out Chef Jose's apple pie à la mode. The judges had eliminated Chef Tony, who had baked brownies.

* * * *

With the pistol in her hand, Anna walked down the sidewalk to Ashley's. The apartment door next to hers opened, and Henry stepped out with a cigarette and lighter in his hand.

Fuck. Before she could jump behind the bushes, their eyes locked. Henry reached for his cell, which was clipped to his belt.

She aimed the gun at him. "I wouldn't do that if I were you, Mr. Underwood. Put your hands up."

He glared at her. She needed to be extra careful with the old guy. Henry had been a cop.

"Hands up. Are you deaf or do you just want to die?"

Slowly, he lifted his hands above his head. "Anna, you don't want to do this. This can all be worked out, the way I understand it."

"Really? That's why Sheriff Wolfe has an APB out on me." Things hadn't gone as well as she'd hoped, but now she realized that having Henry's help was needed. No way would Ashley open the door for her. But for Henry the bitch would.

* * * *

Nic's excitement grew as the limo passed the sign that meant he and Sylas were getting close.

"Welcome to Destiny, the best-kept secret in Colorado."

* * * *

Ashley's doorbell rang, startling her awake. She glanced at the new show on her television and realized she must have fallen asleep when the winner of the earlier one had been announced.

The doorbell rang again.

It was almost midnight. *Who could that be at this hour?*

Quietly, she stepped to her door and looked out the peephole. Henry was standing on the other side of her door.

As she turned the lock, she said, "Henry, is everything okay?"

"Don't unlock your door, Ashley," he yelled.

But it was too late.

She heard a muffled sound followed by a loud thud.

Her door swung open.

Anna stood in front of her, holding a gun with a silencer. An unmoving Henry was at her feet on the ground, bleeding.

Panic rolled through Ashley and her heart thudded violently. "Anna, my God, what have you done?" She took a step, trying to reach Henry.

"Get back and shut up, bitch. Put your hands up where I can see them."

"Okay, Anna. Just calm down." Ashley held her hands over her head. "I'll do whatever you say." She couldn't tell if Henry was breathing or not. "But he needs an ambulance."

"Did you not fucking hear me the first time when I told you to shut up?" Anna's eyes were wild and full of hate. "It's his fault. I told him to stay quiet but he had to play the hero." Anna held the gun to Ashley's forehead. "You ruined my life. Now, you're going to pay. Give me the keys to your car. Now."

"My keys are in my purse, Anna." *And so is my gun.* "And my purse is in the bedroom."

"What do you take me for, Ashley? A fool?" Anna glared at her. "I know you carry a gun like everyone else in this hellhole town. Be smart and don't try anything. Now, lead the way to your bedroom."

Her mind was racing like mad. She could tell by the look on Anna's face that the woman wasn't here just for her keys. Anna meant to kill her.

With the barrel of the silencer to her back, Ashley walked down the hallway. She realized that she had no chance of getting her gun out of her purse. But she had to try something. She wasn't about to just roll over and let the psychopath put a bullet in her head.

They stepped into her bedroom. Her purse was on the chair by the door.

With adrenaline coursing through her veins, in one fluid motion, Ashley grabbed her purse and swung it around, trying to knock the gun out of Anna's hand.

It didn't work, but Anna did stumble backward a few steps, giving her a split-second window of opportunity to save herself. Still gripping her purse, she reached inside to get her gun.

Before she was able to pull it out, Anna charged, "You fucking bitch!"

She fell to the floor and her purse flew out of her hand.

Anna was on top of her, pressing her gun between her eyes. A twisted grin appeared on the insane woman's face. "Good-bye, Ashl—"

A vase came crashing over Anna's head, and the woman collapsed on her. Terror stricken, Ashley pushed with all her might, trying to get Anna off of her.

"It's okay, baby." Nic took Anna's gun and lifted the woman off of her.

Sylas bent over her and pulled her into his arms. "She's not going to hurt you."

"You're here," she said with trembling lips. "Both of you."

Their faces were full of concern for her.

She glanced down at Anna, who was out cold on the floor. Even so, Nic still pointed the gun that he'd retrieved at her attacker.

"She wanted to kill me." Her emotions of relief overtook her and she leaned her head into Sylas's chest and began sobbing.

Sylas stroked her hair and held her close.

She opened her eyes. "Oh my God, Henry."

"Nic's calling 9-1-1 now, baby."

Chapter Sixteen

Sylas had his arm around Ashley. She sat between him and Nic in the waiting room of the clinic. The place was packed with the citizens of Destiny concerned for Henry Underwood, who was in surgery.

Phoebe and two of her husbands were in the seats across from him. The sheriff, Phoebe's other husband, had taken Anna to the jailhouse after the bump on her head Nic had given her had been checked out. He squeezed Ashley a little tighter. *I almost lost her tonight.*

The O'Learys sat beside him. They'd been one of the first groups of people to arrive at Ashley's apartment and had been such a support for all of them.

Some of the men who had been part of Nic's intervention were also in the waiting room with their wives.

Nicole Coleman sat with her husbands closest to the door that led to the operating room. Ashley had told him and Nic just how close the deputy sheriff was to Henry. They were like family.

Everyone in the place was concerned about Henry and was praying he would make it through surgery. Sylas had never seen such an outpouring back in Chicago. The people of Destiny cared deeply for one another, and right now all their thoughts were on one man.

Henry had tried to save Ashley, and Anna had shot him in the chest. No one knew if Henry was going to survive the night. In his and Nic's minds and the minds of the entire town, Henry was a hero.

Ethel looked at Ashley. "Are you sure you're okay, sweetie?"

"I'm much better now, especially since my guys came and saved me. Paris took my vitals and everything is back to normal. I'm still a little shaken, but I'll be okay in time to take my exam."

"No way are you taking the bar, honey, after all you've been through." Nic kissed her on the cheek.

Sylas agreed. "You just need to relax until everything is back to normal."

Ashley shook her head. "I'm not going to wait six months for the next time the exam is offered."

Phoebe leaned forward. "I'm with your guys on this one, Ash. You've been through a horrible experience. The bar can wait."

"You of all people know how hard I've studied for this." Ashley took her hand. "You need me to pass the bar. You're going to be a mother. We are still trying to win Jennifer's case. There's so much work that must be done. I want things to go back to normal as much as they can. Taking the bar helps with that. What Henry did…and what my wonderful men did…for me…I want to honor them. I want to make them proud. But most of all I want to take it for myself. I want to prove that I can do it. If I don't, then Anna wins. I am taking the bar."

"God, listen to our girl, Nic. She's so strong." He grabbed her hand and squeezed. "You've already made me proud, sweetheart. I won't stand in your way."

"Neither will I, baby." Nic kissed her. "We're all so proud of you. But Sylas and I will be right there with you."

"With me?" Her eyebrows shot up. "In Denver?"

"Yes, baby," Nic answered.

"Wait a second." Her gorgeous face filled with confusion. "I thought you were both working at Braxton this morning. What are you doing here in Destiny?"

In all the confusion that followed the attack, they hadn't had a chance to tell her.

Nic spread his arms wide. "Surprise, baby."

Sylas grinned and cupped her chin. "It was supposed to be a surprise."

He and Nic told her about the O'Learys sending their plane, about Mr. Jenkins granting them time off, and about how hard it had been for both of them being away from her.

Her eyes lit up. "You don't have to go back to Chicago until my test is over?"

"That's right, sweetheart." Sylas turned to Nic and could sense he was thinking the same thing.

There wasn't a chance they would leave Ashley alone again. One of them would have to stay in Destiny. The other would have to return to fulfill their notice. Who? That would have to be worked out later.

"Oh my God, I can't believe it." She hugged them both. "You can't imagine how much that means to me. I love you both so very much."

"I love you, too, baby." Nic kissed her lightly on the cheek.

"And I love you." He kissed her other cheek.

The door everyone had been staring at swung open.

The doctor went to Nicole. "The surgery was a success. Henry is doing great."

The crowd jumped to their feet and erupted in cheers, hugs, and kisses.

He and Nic held Ashley between them.

"Thank God," she said with tears streaming down her cheeks. "I'm so happy."

"So am I, sweetheart. So am I."

* * * *

Ashley walked down the jailhouse's hallway. Nic and Sylas walked beside her. Sheriff Jason Wolfe was leading them to a room that had dual usage—sometimes to conduct interrogations, sometimes for prisoners to meet with their attorneys—but today there was a brand new usage for the space. The prisoner wanted to speak to *her friend* and victim.

Ashley had been shocked to hear that Anna had requested to meet with her. She'd thought about refusing or at least putting it off until later. Her bar exam was tomorrow and she and her guys were driving to Denver today. But she had been too curious to turn Anna down. What did the woman who had shot Henry, had pushed her way into the apartment, and had been working with Cindy Trollinger want to say?

I have to know.

Nic and Sylas had tried to convince her not to meet with Anna. She'd argued and argued with them to no avail and had begun to think they were right. But it was Sam O'Leary who had convinced the three of them that it might actually be a good idea. "A face-to-face with an attacker can have a very positive impact on a survivor when it is done with those who love and support her by her side."

When the sheriff opened the door, she could feel her heart pounding in her chest. She took a deep breath and walked into the room.

Anna sat at a metal table in handcuffs beside her defense attorney, a man from Goodnight, the most westerly town in the county. "Against my advice, my client wants to speak with you, Ms. Vaughn."

"That is good advice, counselor," she said. "Too bad your client didn't take it."

The sheriff positioned himself by the door, but remained silent.

"I don't care what he says, Ashley. I had to see you. Thank you so much for coming. I wasn't sure you would."

"I almost didn't." She took the middle seat on the other side of the table, and Nic and Sylas took the chairs next to hers. "What do you want from me, Anna?"

"I want you to know I'm sorry. Sorry for everything." But the woman's demeanor didn't hold an ounce of sincere remorse or guilt for the horror she'd done.

"This is an act. You and I both know it. You're going to be convicted. Stop trying to get your sentence reduced. You will find no sympathy from me."

"It's not like that, Ashley. We're friends, you and I. Cindy Trollinger threatened me. She said if I didn't do what she wanted that she would kill me. That's the only reason I did what I did."

She pounded her fists on the surface of the table. "What you did, Anna, was shoot Henry."

"I didn't mean to."

"That's complete and utter BS. You know it, and I know it. And after you shot poor Henry, you meant to kill me."

Anna's act continued. "It's not true. I swear it."

"Nothing you say now or later will convince me otherwise. I was there. Remember? I saw and heard everything. You put a gun to my head and told me that I ruined your life and that I was going to pay."

"You don't understand."

"I understand a whole bunch more than you give me credit for. What did Trollinger promise you? Why did she have you enter that virus into the law office's computer?"

"Don't answer those questions," her attorney said.

"No. I don't want to hold back anything. If this helps bring that bitch down, then I want to help. She only promised not to kill me."

Ashley could tell that was a lie.

Anna continued. "But I know that she wanted Jennifer Steele's ranch. She had gotten a man to pose as Walter Steele. Trollinger had access to confidential information that reported how much natural gas sits under the Steele Ranch. It's worth hundreds of millions of dollars."

It seemed that Anna was actually telling the truth to Ashley now. If accurate, Trollinger's motive was clear. Greed. Anna's claim connected Trollinger to the Steele Ranch case, but Ashley needed proof. Concrete proof. "What information? Where is it?"

"I don't know. I swear. I saw it on her desk when we met."

Once again, it seemed to her that Anna was telling the truth. "What about the imposter? Who is he?"

"I don't know. I met him in Trollinger's office. He had a thick Cajun accent."

Cajun accent? Louisiana? Not Florida? That was important to remember. "What else?"

Anna shook her head. "That's all I know, Ashley. If I knew anything else I would tell you."

"You know more. That's as obvious to me as it gets." She leaned over the table. "And I bet Trollinger didn't threaten you."

Frowning, Anna squirmed in her chair. She was getting agitated.

"She promised to cut you in on all that money, didn't she?"

"Shut up, Ashley."

Ashley stood, and Nic and Sylas rose, staying protectively by her side. It gave her strength and courage to continue. "And you were stupid and believed her."

"I said shut up."

Anna's attorney stood, clearly trying to get control of the room. "This meeting is over."

"Fuck you, asshole," Anna spat at him and then turned back to her. "You don't know a goddamn thing, bitch."

"We should leave," Sylas said through clenched teeth while Nic glared at Anna.

Her attacker's words had enraged both of them.

"It's okay, guys," Ashley told them as calmly as she could muster. "Just give me a minute."

"Honey, I really think we should go," Nic said. "She's out of control."

"There's nothing she can do to me, and I still have things I need to say to her."

"But we don't want you to have to go through this, sweetheart," Sylas said.

She touched him on the cheek and grabbed Nic's hand. "It's really okay. Sam was right about everything. I actually feel much better." She turned back to Anna. "After you did Trollinger's dirty work, she cut you loose. You were worthless to her. Just trash to set out to the curb."

"I'll kill you. I swear it."

"No, you won't, Anna. We're not friends. You don't have any friends." Ashley walked to the door with her wonderful men, who were holding her hand, giving her their support. "I am going to testify for the prosecution on your case. I hope they throw away the key."

Once they were in the hallway, the sheriff shut and locked the door, leaving the ranting Anna and her frustrated attorney behind.

"I'm so proud of you, baby." Nic put his arm around her.

Sylas kissed her tenderly on the cheek. "You handled yourself so well."

"She sure did." Sheriff Wolfe smiled. "That was very impressive, Ashley. You're going to make quite the lawyer."

"Thanks, Jason."

There was a loud buzzing sound.

The sheriff laughed. "I guess her attorney is ready to get away from Anna, too. Good luck with the bar. I'll see you later. I need to put Anna back in her cell."

When they walked out of the jailhouse, Ashley brought out her phone. "Guys, we have a lot of work to do on the Steele case."

"We also have to get you to Denver, baby," Nic said, opening her car door.

Sylas sat in the back and Nic got behind the wheel.

"I know, but we can make calls on the drive? Jennifer is depending on us. I've got to call Jena and let her know what we learned in there about Jennifer's case. Sylas, you call Phoebe and tell her everything."

Sylas nodded.

"Before we head down the road, I need to make a call, too." Nic brought out his phone. "I know a geologist that will be able to tell us if Anna's claim about the natural gas on the ranch is true."

"That's fantastic." She realized how great it was going to be to work with Nic and Sylas at the law office. They were incredible attorneys.

"Hi, Ashley," Jena's voice came through her cell.

"Jena, I have some news about Walter Steele you need to hear. Anna just confirmed that he is an imposter. We need to be searching records in Louisiana for him."

Chapter Seventeen

Nic finished reading the information from the Energy Information Administration. His geologist friend was the one who discovered the two-year-old report that had been buried at the agency.

He and Sylas were sitting in a café in Denver across from the building where Ashley was finishing her bar exam. Sylas was on the phone with Jena, getting an update.

Nic looked at the time on his cell. Ashley would be walking into the café any minute. She'd been very pleased and confident after completing the first part of the test yesterday. He had no doubt she would feel the same way today.

Sylas ended his call with Jena.

"Sylas, take a look at this." He turned his laptop on the café's table so that Sylas could see his screen.

"Oh my God, Anna wasn't lying. How much are the gas reserves valued at with today's prices?"

"Five hundred to six hundred million. That definitely has to be Trollinger's motive."

"Be sure to let your geologist buddy know how much we appreciate him."

"I owe him a bottle of scotch, but it was Jena and her husbands who discovered the Trollinger connection."

"Maybe we should send them a couple of bottles, Nic."

"Definitely. Without them we wouldn't know that Trollinger paid off that EIA clerk to hide the Steele Ranch file." The guy had been arrested but didn't have any clue how to find Trollinger. "This improves our position with the case but we still need more. How's Jena's research with the Louisiana records going?"

"Walter Steele's identity hasn't been disproved yet, I'm afraid. She's still digging, though. I'm sure she'll find something."

"None of this would be happening if it weren't for our girl, Sylas."

He nodded. "She is brilliant, that's for sure. You know that we are going to have our hands full at Phase Four with her."

"But there's no one else I want my hands on, bro."

"Me either. When's your first lesson with Zac?"

"Tomorrow." What he'd learned from Sylas and Ashley during the drive to Denver about the life intrigued and excited him. He couldn't wait to get started on his training as a Dom. "If it weren't for Mr. Jenkins, I would be leaving for Chicago tonight."

"He's a good man. Let's send him a bottle, too."

They had contacted Mr. Jenkins and told him what had happened to Ashley with Anna. When Nic offered to extend his notice another two weeks to allow Sylas to remain in Destiny with Ashley, Mr. Jenkins thanked both of them but declined the offer. In fact, he had insisted that they stay with Ashley. "I've never worked with finer men than the two of you. Forget your notice. Your last day at the office, gentlemen, was this past Friday, but I'll make sure you are paid until the end of the month. Don't worry about Braxton. We'll be fine. You take care of Ms. Vaughn."

"Here she comes." Sylas motioned to the café's entrance. "And with a big smile on her face."

Nic stood and turned to the door.

She ran into his and Sylas's arms. "I did it. I'm finished. And I think I nailed it."

* * * *

Ashley took the cup of coffee from the new paralegal. "Thanks, Erin."

Erin handed Jena a cup as well.

"I sure need this," Jena said. "Thanks."

She, Erin, and Jena had been working non-stop trying to find something, anything, that would prove the man claiming to be Walter Steele was an imposter. So far, nothing.

"I finished going through the stack of files you gave me this morning, Ms. Vaughn...I mean, Ashley."

"You'll get used to it, Erin. This office is very casual." She liked Erin and knew the twenty-four year old was going to fit in perfectly. "Did you find anything that might help with the Steele Ranch case?"

"Sorry to say I didn't. Nothing suspicious. Walter Steele has lived in Florida for over fifty years."

"That fits the timeline when Bill's brother left Destiny. What else?"

"He was a handyman in the town. He does have a record. Several counts of public intoxication and multiple DUIs. He hasn't had a driver's license in years. Before buying that condo a year ago, he lived at the Sleepy Moon Motel for fifteen years."

"No way his story is true," Jena said. "How the hell does a handyman who is only paid in cash and has never filed a tax return save enough cash to buy a two-hundred-thousand-dollar condo? The only answer that makes any sense is Cindy Trollinger gave him the cash."

"But we don't have any proof. What else, Erin?"

"Prior to that, Mr. Steele rented a room from a man who has since died. I called the manager at the motel. He corroborated Mr. Steele's story. I also got in touch with people Mr. Steele has worked for. Mrs. Emily Cotton told me that Mr. Steele has been doing work for her family since the 1970s. He's never claimed to be anyone but Walter Steele."

"And of course her family paid him in cash like everyone else, right?"

"Yes, Ashley," Erin said. "That's what Mrs. Cotton told me."

"No tax records with a social security number to check. No wonder he hasn't ever filed an income tax return."

"We can turn this over to the IRS, but it won't help with our case, will it?" Jena asked.

"No. Damn. I really can't understand this." Ashley's frustration continued to build. "I don't buy it. The only records on a fifty-eight-year-old man are a birth certificate, some real estate papers, and a property tax filing."

"Maybe Anna was lying," Jena said. "I've scoured the records in Louisiana, and haven't found anything to help us."

"We should have found something on the man by now." Ashley closed her eyes, recalling what Anna had said.

He had a thick Cajun accent. What are we missing?

"All we can do is keep digging. Something has to surface we can use." Ashley sent a text to Phoebe, who was currently in court on another case, about the little they'd uncovered.

She was surprised when a text came back.

In recess for the rest of the day on this one. I'm on my way back to the office. Ash, we need more. Keep digging.

Will do. And when Nic and Sylas get back from their lesson at Phase Four, I'll put them on the search with Jena and me. We need all hands on deck on this one, Phoebe.

They didn't have much time. Jennifer's hearing was set for next week.

Chapter Eighteen

Sylas sat next to Phoebe in the Swanson County Courthouse. Nic sat on the other side of him. Their client, Jennifer Steele, was in the chair next to Nic.

Mrs. Cotton was on the stand and one of the plaintiff's attorneys was questioning her.

Walter Steele, or the man claiming to be Walter Steele, sat with his other high-dollar attorneys at the opposing counsel's desk.

Things weren't looking good for Jennifer, despite the endless hours of research. He and Nic hadn't had much alone time with Ashley since the move to Destiny. This case had demanded most of their focus. Except for the few hours of training he and Nic had gone through at Phase Four with Zac, every other waking hour had been spent searching thousands of records in the hopes of finding the needle in the haystack. But the elusive needle hadn't been found.

Ashley and Jena were at this very moment at the law office on their laptops. They were working feverishly in a last-ditch effort to find something that would help Jennifer. But time was running out.

Sylas loved Ashley's never-give-up attitude. They had checked every record possible in Louisiana and Florida. What else could there be?

"Mrs. Cotton, could you point out for the court the man you know as Walter Steele?"

"I certainly can." Mrs. Cotton was seventy-three and had a warm smile. She pointed at the imposter. "That's Walter Steele."

"Please let the record show that Mrs. Cotton identified the plaintiff as Walter Steele," the lawyer said.

"He certainly is Walter," the woman continued. "He's worked for me and my family for years. One of the finest men I know."

"Just answer the question, Mrs. Cotton." Wearing her judge's robe, Ethel presided over the court with a firm hand.

"Thank you, Mrs. Cotton. Your witness." Walter Steele's attorney took his seat.

Phoebe rose from her chair and came around the table. "Mrs. Cotton, did Mr. Steele have a nickname?"

"Not that I'm aware of, but my late husband did call him 'Walt.' "

"Do you know Mr. Steele's middle name?"

"I don't."

Things were looking really bad for their case.

"No further questions, Your Honor."

* * * *

Staring at her laptop's screen, Ashley felt every tick of the clock. They were running out of time.

"Anything?" Jena was also typing away on her own laptop.

"No. Damn. What are we missing?"

"I wish I knew, Ashley. The only thing we've got is Anna said he had a Cajun accent. But you've seen the recorded deposition. He doesn't have one now."

Cajun accent. That's the key.

Ashley typed in "Cajun accent" in her browser. The pages brought up were a Wikipedia article and some YouTube videos. Nothing helpful. She clicked on the Wikipedia article. There was a map of Louisiana on the right side of the page with the counties highlighted where the dialect was spoken the most. But she and Jena had checked those counties and all the other counties in the state.

What are we missing?

She looked at the map again.

A text came in from Nic. *Walter Steele is taking the stand now.*

"Damn it." She told Jena Nic's message.

"I'm sorry, Ashley. I wish we could have found something."

"Wait." She looked at the map of Louisiana on her screen. "That's got to be it." She typed a new search into her browser. *Where can the Cajun accent be heard?*

The page that appeared was an article by a professor of linguistics at Tulane titled "The Geography of the Cajun Accent."

She scanned the man's research and nearly jumped for joy when she read, "many Creoles and Cajuns migrated to Southeast Texas, and in especially large numbers in the Beaumont and Port Arthur area."

"We've been looking in the wrong state, Jena." She showed her the article.

Jena nodded and went to work. Most states required a fee to get a copy of a birth certificate, whether electronic or in print. Texas was no exception. But Jena had skills to get around that. Two minutes later they were looking at the birth certificate of the man they'd been trying to find for weeks.

"Text Nic." Ashley jumped out of her chair. What they'd found wasn't enough to win the case, but with the right cross-examination of the imposter, it could be. "Tell him I'm coming."

"I will. Go."

She nodded and ran out the door. Her mind was racing as fast as her feet.

Walter David Steele, not Walter Leon Steele.

She passed the Black Dragon statue and continued running through the park.

Born February 9th in Beaumont, not August 11th in Destiny.

The man suing Jennifer for the ranch was an imposter. It all fit now. Trollinger had found the man in Florida. Only three years older than Bill Steele's brother, so the age wouldn't be hard to disprove. He also had very few records on file. The only difference was their initials, and that wouldn't have been found out had she not printed a copy of the property tax record with the man's real initial. Trollinger must have realized the mistake and corrected it. How she was able to get official records changed still baffled Ashley, but Jena assured her it could be done.

But even with this new birth certificate, we won't win unless we can trip the man up during the cross.

Out of the corner of her eye, she saw the Green Dragon statue, which was said to bring luck. Ashley whispered a prayer for Jennifer as she ran out of the park, crossed East Street, and hurried up the courthouse steps.

* * * *

Nic saw Ashley, a little disheveled, enter the courtroom. He'd shown Jena's text to Sylas and Phoebe a moment ago. Ashley and Jena had found a birth certificate that gave them a reason to hope.

"Mr. Steele, why did you leave your hometown of Destiny and your brother?" The plaintiff's lawyer looked so smug.

Walter Steele smiled. "I was just a young man and thought I knew everything."

Ashley moved next to Phoebe and placed a copy of the birth certificate on the table. She whispered, "Did you get Jena's text?"

"We did." Phoebe scanned the certificate and passed it to him and Sylas. "This isn't an official copy, Ash."

The imposter continued to drone on and on. "I decided to take off on my own. I moved to Florida and started my life. My brother and I were close. Very close."

"We could ask the judge for a stay on the grounds of this new information," Sylas suggested quietly. "We could get an official copy by tomorrow. It's new evidence."

"I doubt the judge would grant us a stay, and even if she did give it to us I believe it would ruin our advantage," he told them.

Phoebe leaned forward. "How would it ruin our advantage, Nic? Our position isn't very good right now."

"We'd have to disclose this to his counsel and what do we really have? How do we prove that this birth certificate is the plaintiff's?"

Walter Steele slammed his fists on the rail. "And then suddenly my brother stopped calling and writing. I never knew why until recently when I learned he married her." The man pointed his crooked finger at Jennifer.

"Please let the record show that Mr. Steele is referring to the defendant, Mrs. William Steele," his lawyer said. "Please go on."

There was fire in Ashley's eyes. "The best way to prove this is that bastard's certificate is to get him to admit it, Phoebe. During your cross you could trip him up."

Phoebe's eyes narrowed. "My cross?"

"Yours, or Nic's, or Sylas's. Whoever. Just hit Trollinger's imposter hard and don't let up."

Nic was impressed at the passion Ashley was showing.

The bastard on the stand shook his head. "That woman must've been the reason my brother never reached out to me again. I wouldn't have known that he died if I hadn't tried to look him up on the Internet at the library last year. That's when I realized why she'd kept us apart. She wanted my family's ranch all for herself."

"Objection, your honor." Phoebe stood. "Conjecture."

"Sustained," Ethel said.

"No further questions, your honor." The attorney took his seat. "Your witness."

"One moment, your honor, while I confer with my associates."

"Do you need a recess?"

Phoebe shook her head. "No, your honor. Just one moment."

Ethel nodded.

Phoebe turned to Ashley. "You're up."

"What? Me?"

"You clearly have an idea of how to cross the man. You're the one who found this certificate."

"But Jennifer is depending on this," Ashley said.

"And that's exactly the reason you're going to do the cross."

Ashley turned to him and Sylas. "You agree with this?"

"She's the boss, but yes," Sylas said. "You're ready."

Jennifer smiled. "Ashley, I would be honored to be the first client you represented in court."

"Go, baby." Nic grabbed her hand and squeezed. "Win this case."

"I've very nervous, but okay." Ashley walked around the desk and stepped up to the stand.

Nic leaned forward, all his focus on the woman of his dreams.

She smiled. "Hi, Mr. Steele. That was quite a sad story, losing your family like that."

"Yes it was, miss. Very sad."

"Are you nervous, Mr. Steele? I certainly am. You're the very first person I've ever addressed in court. I just got my license."

"Good for you. I feel honored that I'm your first one, and yes, I am a little nervous."

"We'll just go through this together. I understand you and your brother were very close."

"We sure were."

"What did you all do when you were kids?"

"Objection," his attorney said. "Relevance, your honor."

"Your honor, my line of questioning is important and will become clear if I'm allowed to continue."

"I'll allow it, counselor, for the moment. Overruled."

"Thank you." Ashley turned back to the plaintiff. "Where were we, Mr. Steele?"

"You asked me what my brother and I did when we were kids?"

"That's right."

Nic was so impressed by how Ashley had control of the man. He was repeating her words back to her. He leaned over to Sylas and quietly said, "Our girl is one helluva good lawyer."

Sylas nodded. "She sure is."

"Bill and I did the normal things. We fished. Camped out. Rode bikes."

"You fished?"

"We sure did."

"What kinds of things did you fish for, Walter? Perch, crawdads, crappie?"

"Yep. All of them."

"Objection, your honor." His attorney stood.

"Overruled," Ethel snapped back.

"But, Your Honor—"

"I said 'overruled.' Now sit down." Ethel glared at the man.

He shrugged and returned to his chair.

"Continue," she told Ashley.

"Mr. Steele, you and your brother didn't use fishing poles to catch the crawdads, did you?"

He laughed. "No, young lady. You need a net for crawdads."

"There's nothing better than a crawfish boil, is there, Mr. Steele?"

"I've got an *envie* for some crawfish, *sha*."

"I detect a little Cajun accent there. Did you live in Louisiana or Beaumont?"

"Beaumont…I mean…I visited Beaumont before."

Nic saw the man was rattled. *Good job, baby. Now take him out.*

Ashley leaned forward. "Your name is Walter David Steele, correct?"

"Yes, that's right."

"I'm confused." Ashley stepped to the desk and got a copy of the original filing of the case. "It says here your name is Walter Leon Steele."

The man wiped his brow. "That's my name."

"Wait. Which is it?"

"Leon."

Nic was so proud of Ashley. He'd never seen any attorney conduct a cross exam as well as she was. *This is her first time. Wow.*

"You just had a birthday, Mr. Steele, didn't you?"

"I *shore* did."

Ashley smiled. "You turned fifty-seven, didn't you?"

"Yes, ma'am. Lived a long life, I did, *sha.*"

"What day is your birthday?"

"February 9th."

Ashley's sweet demeanor changed and she glared at the man. "You, sir, are not William Steele's brother. William Steele's brother was born August 11th and if the real Walter Steele were still alive he would only be turning fifty-four. That's three years younger than you are, sir."

"Objection, your honor. Leading the witness."

"Overruled."

"Mr. Steele, you are under oath. You can be sent to jail for lying."

"I don't want to go to jail, young lady. I'm sorry. She told me if I would say these things she would buy me a condo. And she did, *sha.*"

"Who told you to lie?"

"Ms. Trollinger."

"Objection, your honor."

"Overruled. Sit down now or you will be in contempt."

"Mr. Steele, would you please tell the court your full name and where you were born."

"I am Walter David Steele. I was born in Beaumont, Texas, fifty-seven years ago. I have no claim to the Steele Ranch, *sha.* I'm sorry."

Ashley addressed Ethel, and in a confident tone said, "Your honor, in light of Mr. Steele's admission that he is not Walter Leon Steele, I ask that this case be dismissed."

"Granted. Because of the plaintiff's own testimony, this case is dismissed." Ethel pounded her gavel.

Ashley turned around.

Jennifer was the first to get to her, wrapping her arms around Ashley. "You did it. Thank you. Thank you."

Phoebe shook hands with the opposing counsel and then moved to congratulate Ashley. "Ash, you blew me away. You were wonderful."

"I'm just glad we won." Her smile was so beautiful to behold.

"I've seen more seasoned lawyers crack under lesser cross examinations, but you held your own with Mr. Steele." Sylas kissed her on the cheek. "How does it feel to have won your first case, sweetheart?"

"I really did win it, didn't I?"

Nic pulled her in tight. "You *shore* did."

Chapter Nineteen

Enjoying another wonderful meal at the Colorado Skies Steakhouse, Ashley sat between Nic and Sylas in the private room Jennifer had reserved for the crowd. And what a crowd it was.

Jena and her two husbands, Matt and Sean, were to their left. The O'Learys sat to their right. Across from them were Phoebe and her three husbands, Jason, Mitchell, and Lucas. And rounding out the group were Jennifer and Erin, each sitting at opposite ends of the table.

Brett and Adam, who she'd seen on the date with Nic and Sylas, walked in with the champagne Jennifer had ordered.

"Jennifer, this is too much." Phoebe shook her head. "Five bottles of Dom Pérignon?"

Jennifer laughed. "To start with. This is a celebration. I also ordered a bottle of sparkling apple juice for you, Phoebe."

The entire town was thrilled with the news about the Wolfe's twins. Keeping secrets in Destiny was difficult, but she was glad that Phoebe still hadn't found out about her surprise baby shower.

Adam filled their glasses.

Jennifer stood. "A toast to the amazing work of Phoebe and her team. I want to especially thank Jena for all the work she did and Ashley, Destiny's newest lawyer, for getting the imposter to confess on the stand. You saved Bill's and my ranch. I will be forever grateful. Please raise your glasses with me."

"Here. Here," they all said in unison, and took a sip of the delicious beverage.

Sam stood. "A toast to the expectant parents. All of us in this room can't wait to meet your twins."

"Don't rush it, Sam." Phoebe smiled. "I still have a wedding dress I need to fit into next week."

Everyone laughed.

Sam grinned. "To your babies." He lifted his glass.

"Here. Here."

Patrick tapped his knife to his glass. "Before you sit, I'd like to give a toast as well." He turned to Ethel.

The love in his eyes for his wife warmed Ashley's heart.

"Sweetheart, I have to say you sure looked sexy in your judge's robes today."

"Patrick Michael O'Leary, can you be serious?" Ethel grinned.

"Thank you for putting up with Sam and me all these years. Our love continues to grow each and every day. To the love of my life."

They all toasted them.

Ethel kissed her husbands and looked at Ashley. "Since we're all toasting, I'd like to offer one for this amazing young woman. Congratulations on your first victory in the courtroom. I have no doubt that there will be many more. Only one other attorney has ever impressed me as much as you did today, Ashley. And she happens to be the senior partner at the newly named Wolfe and Vaughn Law Offices. Ashley. Phoebe. I expect great things from both of you."

Everyone cheered and took another sip of champagne.

More toasts followed until everyone was honored.

"I don't know about the rest of you," Erin said, "but can we slow down on the toasts? I'm getting a little light headed."

"Just one more," Sylas said.

He and Nic stood and turned to Ashley.

"Sweetheart, you are the most wonderful woman in the world," Sylas said.

"Guys, I've already been toasted tonight."

"We know," they said in unison.

"But this is really important to us, baby." Nic sat his glass down on the table, and he and Sylas got down on their knees.

The shock caused her to bring her hands up, covering her mouth. "Oh my God…you're not…?"

"We are," they answered, once again in unison.

Each of them took one of her hands.

"As I was saying before," Sylas said. "You are the most wonderful woman in the world. I fell in love with you in Chicago, but it was here in Destiny that I realized that I wanted to spend the rest of my life with you. Your dreams are my dreams. Your wants are my wants. We belong together." He squeezed her hand. "I love you with all my heart, Ashley. Would you do me the honor of becoming my wife?"

"Yes, Sylas. I will marry you. I love you so much."

He kissed her deeply.

"Ashley, I almost lost you," Nic said in a serious tone. "I love absolutely everything about you, baby. The way you crinkle your nose when you're thinking. How your eyebrow shoots up when I've teased you too much. And I never tire of seeing how passionate you are when you are fighting for a just cause. What a fool I was back in Chicago, but no more. Like Sylas said, your dreams are my dreams. Your wants, my wants. I'm a better man because you are in my life. I followed you to Destiny, not realizing that *you* were my destiny. Spend the rest of your life with me and Sylas. I love you, Ashley. Will you marry me?"

"Yes. Of course I'll marry you. I love you, honey."

As he kissed her, she could hear the cheers from the others.

Sylas held a ring in front of her. Nic held her hand up and he slipped it on her finger.

"It's beautiful." The diamond sparkled in her eyes. "When did you find time to get this? We've been so busy with Jennifer's case."

"We bought it when were in Chicago," Sylas said. "We knew that we wanted to spend the rest of our lives with you, sweetheart."

"Together," Nic added with a smile. "I may be an old dog, but you can teach me new tricks."

"Me, too," Sylas said. He leaned in close and whispered, "And Nic and I can't wait to show our bride-to-be some of the tricks we've been learning at Phase Four."

A delicious shiver ran up and down her spine.

Everyone congratulated them as Adam brought in their first of many courses.

As they enjoyed the meal, Ashley kept glancing at her ring. *I'm engaged.* She looked at her two fiancés. *My husbands-to-be and my Doms. I can't wait to see what they've learned.*

* * * *

As the three of them stepped up to Ashley's front door, Sylas cupped her chin. "Give me your keys, sub."

"Yes, Master." She reached in her purse and produced the keys.

"Look at the red in her cheeks, bro." Nic stood next to him. "She's excited about what we have in store for her. My God, our fiancée is beautiful."

"Yes, she is." Even though they'd only been engaged for a couple of hours, Sylas knew their whole world had changed—changed for the better. She was his and Nic's future. They were a family. He unlocked the door and swung it open. "Go to your bedroom. Take off everything but your stilettos. Then I want you to come out to your living room and give Master Nic and I a parade. Do you understand?"

Her sexy grin appeared on her face. "Yes, Master. I understand." She rushed into her bedroom and shut the door.

"How do you think I'm doing, Nic? Did I sound commanding enough?"

"I think so, but I'm not a sub, bro." Nic laughed. "When she comes out, I'll give it a try. See how I sound."

"Good idea, Nic." Sylas couldn't contain his excitement. "She's wearing our ring, bro."

"Yes, she is. She's going to be our wife. This night just keeps getting better and better." Nic frowned. "Shit. I forgot the satchel. Be right back. Don't start without me."

Nic ran out the door to retrieve the bag they'd filled with sex toys.

She said yes. He would remember this night for the rest of his life.

Nic returned with the satchel just as Ashley came out of her bedroom as she had been commanded, naked and in stilettos.

"Oh my God, you look beautiful, sweetheart," Nic said. "I'm so in love with you."

Sylas placed his hand on Nic's shoulder. "That's real commanding, bro."

They both grinned and Ashley giggled.

"Something funny, sub?" Nic's voice deepened with a slight threat to it, as Zac had taught them.

Ashley's eyes widened and she trembled. "No, Sir."

He sensed she was excited and anxious, which was the perfect mix of emotions that would allow them to give her more pleasure. "Telling a lie to your Masters is going to earn you some slaps to that gorgeous ass. You thought something was funny, didn't you?"

"I-I was just...I mean...when you said—"

Her nervousness ramped up his lust. "You were naughty then, weren't you, sub?"

Ashley clasped her hands together, looked down at the floor, and nodded. "Yes, Master. I was naughty."

"What happens to subs when they are naughty?" Nic asked.

"They get in trouble with their Doms, Master." Her voice shook slightly with what sounded to him like uneasiness and expectancy.

"Come here," Sylas commanded her, taking a seat on her sofa.

She moved slowly and stood in front of him. He could smell her desire wafting from her.

He'd learned that a sub's anticipation of a punishment was often more intense than the actual punishment itself. With that in mind, he decided to tell her what he intended to do before doing it. "You deserve to be spanked, don't you?"

"Yes, Master. I do." Her breasts rose and fell from her shallow breathing.

"Because you decided to laugh, both your Doms are going to spank you."

"I'm sorry, Sir." Her lower lip began to quiver.

He grabbed her hands. "I know you are, but you still have to learn your lesson, sweetheart. How many licks should I give you?"

"One, Master. Please. Just one."

He grinned. It was clear to him that she would hardly be satisfied with a single slap to her ass. She was trying to negotiate her punishment down by trying to sound innocent and contrite. *A ploy? Most definitely.*

"It's going to be more than one, sub. That's for sure. Three?"

She was so sexy standing naked in her high heels in front of him with a pleading look on her face.

"Not three, Sylas. She needs five from you and five from me."

"I agree, bro." He pulled her on top of his lap, face down, stretching her out on the sofa. He caressed her ass and could feel her trembles. His cock hardened. "First one, sub. Here it comes. Are you ready?"

"Yes, Master."

With lightning speed, he slapped the center of her curvy backside.

She moaned, which spurred him on.

Another slap to her soft ass landed on her right cheek. He reached under her and caressed her pussy, which was already dampening. Feeling her wetness on his fingers caused fire to pulse in his veins.

"How many more from my hand is left for you, sub?"

"Three more, Master," she answered with quivers in her voice.

"That's right." He slapped her left cheek and marveled at the pink color that was popping up on her ass. He spanked her two more times, and was rewarded with her moans. He felt her pussy, which was drenched with her cream. It took every bit of self-control inside him to keep from taking her right then and right there.

"Nic, your turn to paint our sub's ass pink." He lifted her off the couch, coming to his feet.

She wrapped her hands around his neck and leaned her head into his chest.

Nic took the same position he had on the couch, and he lowered Ashley down onto Nic's lap.

Watching Nic spank her drove him wild. There was no jealousy inside him, only awe and desire. Nic's slaps came faster than his, one right after the other. The sound made from the collisions of his hand to her ass echoed in the room.

"Let's take our pretty little sub to the bedroom, Sylas." Nic rose from the sofa with their sub in his arms.

"Agreed." Sylas picked up the satchel and followed them.

Nic placed her in the center of the bed and kissed her on the forehead.

Ashley still wore her stilettos, which Sylas found incredibly sexy.

Her entire body was flushed with desire. She stared at both of them with longing in her eyes.

He and Nic stripped out of their clothes. Freeing his cock and balls from his jeans and underwear didn't give him any relief but only made him even hungrier for her. He pulled out the two sets of handcuffs they'd brought and tossed one set to Nic.

As they'd planned before the dinner, they each took one of her hands and attached it to the headboard of her bed, stretching her arms wide apart.

As Nic brought out the vibrator from the satchel, he slipped the blindfold over her eyes.

"Look at our sub, Nic. Have you ever seen anyone more beautiful in your life?"

"Never." Nic flipped the vibrator's switch. It began to hum and Ashley began to squirm.

He smiled. *Anticipation.* "You know what is causing that sound, sweetheart?"

"Yes, Master. A vibrator." Her breathing was labored.

"That's right, baby," Nic said. "Very good. Do you like it on low or fast?"

"Low on my breasts and fast on my pussy, Sir."

"You want the low setting here, sub?" Nic pinched her nipples, rolling the little buds between his thumb and forefinger.

"Oh God, yes. Please."

Sylas got the bottle of lubricant out of the satchel and began slicking up his fingers.

Clicking the vibrator on high, Nic whispered in her ear, "And fast here?" With his hand, he pressed on her clit.

"Yes, Masters. Please. Please."

Nic turned the vibrator back to low and touched her nipples with it. "You like that, baby?"

"Oh yes. So much. So good."

Sylas fingered her anus with his slicked-up fingers. "I'm going to fuck this gorgeous ass of yours and make you squirm, sub." He sent one digit past her tight ring, stretching her flesh, making her ready to receive his cock.

She panted out her excitement. "Ohhh."

When Nic clicked the vibrator on high, Sylas saw her toes curl.

"I want you so bad, Masters," she confessed. "Please. I need you inside me."

He looked at Nic and mouthed the word "anticipation," a word that had been repeated over and over to them during their lessons. It was nearly impossible to hold back, but he knew the longer they waited the more pleasure she would feel.

Nic nodded and placed the tip of the vibrator on her clit.

"Oh God. Oh God. Oh God. I can't wait. I'm going to come."

He stopped fingering her ass. "Do not come until we say so, sub."

Nic removed the vibrator from her pussy and clicked it off. "Do you understand, sub? You come when we say so and not before."

"I'll try, Masters, but it's so...so..." She took a deep breath. "So intense. I'm not sure I'll be able to stop. Spank me if you must, but that's the truth."

"Our little vixen." Nic grinned. "She's deserves her reward, don't you think?"

"I agree." *Dom or not, I can't hold back any longer myself.*

They removed her handcuffs and blindfold.

Together they lifted her off the bed and held her between them, Nic in the front and him in the back.

Nic held her thighs, while he grabbed onto her waist. She wrapped her arms and legs around Nic and leaned her head back into him. It took a few heavy breathing moments for him and Nic to get the hang of how to take her in this position simultaneously, but they did—and it felt incredible.

He pushed into her ass slowly, feeling her tighten on his cock and hearing her throaty pants in his ears.

Nic thrust into her pussy, and she began trembling between them.

"Yes. Yes. Yes." Her cries of passion inflamed his hot desires.

"You. Want. More. Sub?" Each of Nic's syllables had a primal tone, like the beat of a native's drum.

"Please, Master. Please. More. More. More."

He and Nic's thrusts into her synched up perfectly and they began to go faster and faster. Deeper and deeper. In and out.

She writhed between them like captured prey. "Masters, I can't hold back any longer."

"Don't hold back, sweetheart." Sylas breathed into her ear, continuing to plunge into her ass. "Come for us."

"Yes, baby," Nic growled. "Come. Let go. I want to feel your cream all over my cock."

"Coming. Coming. Coming." She clawed, nipped, and yelled as she climaxed.

Nic's eyes closed and he groaned, reaching orgasm.

Sylas thrust one last time into Ashley's ass, and his cock released the warm liquid into her body.

Ashley's breathing softened after a few minutes. "That was incredible. I love you both so very much."

"I love you, baby." Nic stroked her hair. "You're amazing."

"I love you, sweetheart." Sylas kissed her lush lips. "We forgot something, Nic."

"We did?"

He nodded. "We forgot to set up safe words."

"I didn't think about it either," Ashley said. "You two took my breath away. But I'm sure you understand the word stop. And of course I didn't have to use it. You both made me feel so comfortable. I trust you completely."

"So what should we choose as your safe word, baby?" Nic asked.

"I was thinking 'Chicago' would work for us. It's where we first met."

"And we had some difficult issues to overcome." Sylas vowed to become a full-trained Dom. She deserved his best, and he would throw himself into his training at Phase Four.

Nic certainly was on the same page about their training. "But we did overcome our issues, thank God. I can't live without you, baby."

"Perfect." Sylas ran his hand up and down her arm. Her skin was so soft. "Our word is 'Chicago.' And what about your go word?"

"Do you both know what my favorite dessert is?"

"Molten Lava Cake," they answered in unison.

She laughed. "That's right. How about that?"

"Sweetheart, that's a mouthful," Sylas said.

"No pun intended," Nic added and then burst out laughing.

He and Ashley joined in on the hysterics.

"May only get out 'Molten' or 'Lava' or 'Cake' but you'll know what to do. Just keep on doing whatever you're doing to me."

"What about a caution word?" Nic asked. "When we're pushing you beyond your comfort zone?"

"I'm such a lightweight with wine, as you know, always having to pace myself. How about we use 'Cabernet' for my caution word."

"Love it. Love it. Love it," Nic mocked her teasingly.

She grinned. "I don't always repeat myself like that, do I?"

"Yes, always—when we're making love."

She turned to Sylas. "That's not true, is it?"

"Let's find out, sub." He grabbed her pussy.

"Oh my. Oh my. Oh my." Her mouth formed a perfect *O.* "You're right. I do repeat myself." She giggled.

As his cock began to stiffen again, Sylas stared into the eyes of the woman of his and Nic's dreams. "Nic and I want to make you repeat yourself again and again, sweetheart."

For the rest of our lives.

Chapter Twenty

Ashley filled her plate with more delicious hors d'oeuvres.

Ethel was next to her doing the same. Standing next to Ethel and sipping coffee was Gretchen. The two women, best friends, were in their eighties, but no one would ever know it. Not only did they look twenty years younger, they also had such energy and passion for life. Like all the women of Destiny, Ashley wanted to be just like them.

Ethel sent her a wink. "Your bachelorette party for Phoebe seems to be serving triple duty, Ashley—bachelorette party, baby, and lingerie shower."

"Very true," Gretchen said in her thick British accent, "Just look at how bloody high the two gift tables are stacked. I'm going to tell the hotel staff to bring in another table."

"No you are not," Ethel scolded her. "For once, you're going to just sit back and enjoy yourself. You don't have to wait on anyone. Gretchen Hollingsworth, do you hear me?"

Gretchen laughed and turned to Ashley. "The Irish can be so bossy at times."

Ethel shook her head. "You know I'm not Irish, woman. My husbands are. And stop trying to change the subject. Why do you think Ashley chose to have this party at the hotel? She wanted you to enjoy yourself as much as everyone else."

"Is that true, young lady?"

She smiled and nodded. "I never get much of a chance to talk with you at most of the parties because you are running in and out of the kitchen."

"Well, I appreciate it, Ashley. But half the fun of parties is cooking and taking care of everyone."

Ashley put her arm around the dear woman. "Call me Irish, too, Gretchen, if you must, but you're going to be a princess tonight. Ethel and I are going to see to it. Now, what can I get you?"

Gretchen shrugged. "Someone needs to get another table. Those gifts are going to fall onto the floor."

"I'll go talk to the staff," Ashley said. "But I will be back with a glass of champagne for you. You will drink it and then I'll pour you another."

Ethel laughed. "That's probably the only way we'll get this Brit to relax is to get her drunk."

Gretchen smiled. "That'll be the day."

"I've seen you drunk before, lady," Ethel said. "Don't even deny it."

"Let's talk about something else, please. Like getting that table." Gretchen laughed.

"Now who's being Irish?" Ashley grinned and walked to the door.

"Where you going?" Megan Knight came up beside her. "The party is just getting started."

"I've been instructed to get another table for the gifts."

"Let me guess. Gretchen?"

She nodded and smiled. "The one and only. She was going to get it herself."

"That doesn't surprise me."

"But she finally relinquished the fight and allowed me to get it."

Just then a staff member walked by, and Ashley asked them to get another table.

"How's little Gretchen doing, Megan? She's eight months now, right?"

"She is. Growing like a weed. She's already crawling. Paris says she's a little ahead on her baby skills. Eric and Scott took that to mean Gretchen is going to be a genius."

"They are her daddies and you know how smart they are."

Megan nodded. "Sometimes too smart for their own good, but I love them."

"Will you help me gather up all the ladies? I think we'll have Phoebe open her lingerie gifts first."

"Good idea, Ashley."

Once all the women were seated around Phoebe, Ashley handed her the first gift. "This is from Erica Coleman."

"I hope you like it," Erica said. She was married to Dylan and Cam Strange. They were expecting their first baby. She was just beginning to show.

"I'm sure I'll love it." Phoebe opened the package and pulled out a pair of black crotch-less panties."

The crowd roared.

"I'm sure Jason, Mitchell, and Lucas will love them if she doesn't," Gretchen said with a slight slur. "Oh my. Did I just say that, Ethel?"

"Yes, you did, sweetie. Have another glass of champagne and who knows what else you'll say?"

The laughter continued throughout the evening.

With a slight buzz of her own, Ashley leaned over to Jena and whispered, "Phoebe's getting some very sexy items, isn't she? I especially like that little red teddy that Nicole gave her."

"You do?" Jena grinned. "I'll remember that when we give you *your* shower. Have you set a date yet?"

"Not yet. We've been so busy. Me taking the bar exam. Nic and Sylas's move here. Jennifer's trial. We're just now packing up my apartment."

"I'm so happy for you, Ashley. You've found two wonderful men."

"I have, haven't I?"

"Ashley Vaughn, you devil woman." Phoebe held up her gift for all to see. It was a fishnet dress that didn't leave anything to the imagination. "I love it."

"If you'll notice, it will stretch so you'll be able to wear it your entire pregnancy. I think your guys will appreciate it."

Ashley heard the pounding on the door, her cue to get all the women's attention. "Ladies, there is one more surprise left for Phoebe. Please pull your chairs to the side of the room and get ready for something very special."

"Ash, you've already done so much for me," Phoebe said. "Where should I go?"

"You stay right there in the middle of the room." Ashley motioned to the staff members who were in on the surprise.

The lights dimmed and the music began to play. The doors burst open and the men of Destiny rushed into the room, wearing only leather boots and pants. They began the choreographed dance they'd been practicing in secret for the past several weeks. Nic and Sylas had to learn the steps really fast.

At first, the men danced around Phoebe, with her three guys in the front. But Ashley's eyes never strayed from Nic or Sylas's sexy moves. Phoebe's reaction was perfect. Her cheeks were red and her smile was endearing.

Even though the dance had been Ashley's idea, she had never seen the routine. Halfway through the song, the men broke off and moved to their own wives and girlfriends.

Ashley felt her temperature rise as Nic and Sylas each gave her a lap dance. On cue, like all the men did with their women, Ashley's men grabbed her hands and pulled her onto what was clearly now and for the rest of the night the dance floor. And the party really got underway.

Chapter Twenty-One

Ashley's attendants helped her get into her wedding gown.

The past three months had been a mixed bag of frustration and wonderful—but mostly wonderful.

Ashley shared the frustration of the entire town concerning Cindy Trollinger, who was still at large. Every lead the authorities researched fizzled out. Trollinger had been in Prague last month. When Interpol had arrived at the place she'd been renting, they hadn't find her but found two corpses instead. But Ashley knew that Jason, Jena, Easton Black, and all the members of Shannon's Elite would never give up the search for Destiny's Most Wanted.

I shouldn't be thinking about Trollinger, especially today. Living with Nic and Sylas in Phoebe's rental house had been wonderful, but this evening they would be spending the night in their new home that Lucas had designed and built for them.

Tonight is my honeymoon.

With Phoebe only coming into the office one day a week, she, Nic, and Sylas couldn't leave town. Even with Erin doing such a terrific job, they needed to stay close because of the heavy caseload the firm was balancing.

Ashley had to promise Phoebe she would take off the entire weekend. The only reason Phoebe hadn't argued more was because of the trip to Hawaii that Nic and Sylas had planned for her later in the year.

She actually was glad that her honeymoon was going to be in Destiny. She was excited to begin her new life in her new home with her new husbands.

She stood in front of the full-length mirror and stared at her reflection. The off-the-shoulder gown with its beautiful beading was elegant and beyond timeless. "Wow."

"Oh my God, Ash. You look absolutely stunning." Phoebe sat next to Erica.

"So do you."

"You did a wonderful job picking dresses for the four of us. No one can even tell that Erica and I are pregnant." Phoebe was five months along, and Erica was six. But Doc and Paris estimated that their delivery dates would be close together since twins usually came early. "And just look how glamorous Jena and Desirae are in theirs, too."

"And me, too," Jena's daughter said, twirling around. Kimmie was her flower girl.

"You look very pretty, baby." Jena kissed Kimmie on the forehead.

Sylas's mother—Ashley's soon-to-be mother-in-law—entered the chapel's dressing room. Brenda Hayes had blue eyes, just like Sylas's.

"My goodness, ladies. You all look so beautiful, but especially my Ashley."

Everyone in town had taken to Sylas's parents and his two younger brothers.

"Let me take a good look at you, Mom." She grabbed Brenda's hand and twirled her around. "I think you may steal the show today in this dress."

"I love the color orchid, sweetheart. Have you picked something old to wear yet?" Brenda asked her.

"Oh my gosh. I forgot about all those things. I need three more— old, borrowed, and blue. My dress should count as new, right?"

"Yes, sweetheart. I can help with the old part." Brenda brought out the most beautiful necklace and earrings she'd ever seen. "I'm glad you chose orchid and white for your special day. These match your colors."

She took the jewelry. "Are these alexandrite?"

"Yes. My colors were also orchid and white. Jim bought the necklace and earrings for me to wear on our wedding day. I'd like to give them to you now to wear for your day. That is if you like them."

"I absolutely love them, Mom." She hugged her.

"Good." Brenda wiped her eyes. "I had three boys and now I have a daughter. Ashley, I want you to keep them until you have a daughter of your own."

"Our first tradition. I love it." She put on the earrings and necklace and glanced at her reflection again. "They're perfect. Thank you so much, Mom."

"We only have five minutes," Jena said. "And you still need something blue and something borrowed."

"Here's my pinkie ring, Ash." Phoebe handed it to her. "You can borrow it. Just put it on your right hand."

They could hear the organ begin to play.

Ashley started to panic. "Blue? Blue? There's nothing in this room that's blue."

All the women started digging in their purses.

"Got it." Desirae pulled out a blue headband. "Lift up your dress quick and step into this." Desirae knelt down and pulled the band up to Ashley's thigh, just opposite the other thigh, which had the traditional garter on it. "How does that feel?"

"It's fine," she said. "Thank you, Desirae."

Sylas's dad walked in. "My God, Ashley, aren't you beautiful? I'm so lucky to get to walk you down the aisle to my boys."

"Thanks, Dad. You look very handsome."

"Not bad for a fifty-five-year-old goat. I took a peek at the chapel. It looks like a fairytale fit for a princess."

"Jim, we have the most beautiful princess with us," Brenda said.

"Ashley, I just came from my boys' dressing room." Jim and Brenda's reaction to this wedding had surprised everyone.

They weren't from Destiny, but they were fully accepting and excited about the event. Her mother and father had passed and Nic had never had loving parents before. But now they both did.

"I doubt Nic and Sylas are as nervous as I am."

"They're fit to be tied." Jim kissed the back of her hand. "Your two grooms look so handsome in their white tuxedos, sweetheart. They are going to take your breath away." He smiled and turned to his wife. "Brenda, the ushers are ready to seat you."

"Just one second." With her eyes welling up, Brenda gave her a kiss on the cheek. "I love you."

"I love you, too."

Brenda left and Ashley, her attendants, and her father-in-law walked into the foyer of Destiny's Little Mountain Chapel. Phoebe's husband had designed it. So many weddings were performed here, which was on a mountain overlooking the town.

The organist began playing the wedding march.

Kimmie walked through the double doors down the aisle, followed by Desirae, Jena, and Erica.

Phoebe squeezed Ashley's hand and smiled. Then she followed her other attendants.

"Dad, I'm nervous," she confessed as the butterflies fluttered inside her.

He took her hand. "Don't be. I'm right here beside you."

She nodded and he offered his arm. She took it, holding tight to her bouquet of orchids and white roses.

When the traditional tune that announced the bride's entrance began to play, she heard everyone stand.

When the doors opened, her eyes landed on Nic and Sylas, who were wearing their white tuxedos with their orchid ties.

"Oh my God, Dad," she whispered to him as they took each step. "Look how handsome my grooms are."

"I told you they would take your breath away, sweetheart. Besides, look who their dad is."

She smiled, knowing he was trying to help her relax a little. Brenda had been right. The room did look like a fairytale. She glanced at the people who had come to see her get married. Destiny had to be a ghost town at the moment, since it seemed everyone was here.

Ethel, who was officiating the service, stood at the front. Ashley's attendants stood next to Ethel. The groomsmen were on the other side. Sylas had chosen his two brothers, Kevin and Hunter, to stand with him. Patrick and Sam O'Leary were Nic's groomsmen, who he'd become very close to since his intervention.

Once she and Jim were standing in front, the music stopped.

"Please be seated," Ethel told the crowd, and then she addressed Jim. "Who gives this lovely bride to these two handsome men?"

"I do. It is my pleasure and honor to do so."

Nic and Sylas took her hands, one standing on either side of her. Jim moved to the seat next to Brenda.

Ethel began the ceremony. "We are here because the three of you have decided to join your lives. You come here with precious gifts—mature understanding, your love, your hopes and dreams, your trust in one another, and your faith in life's meaning and purpose, resolved to share life's experiences in enduring love and loyalty. The decision has been made in your hearts and minds, and we are here to witness the public expression of the commitments you have made privately to each other. Marriage is a relationship not to be entered into lightly or thoughtlessly, but reverently, soberly, with deep purposes and in the spirit of enduring love. Much is required of you three. Knowing this, do each of you wish to proceed with this marriage?"

She and her grooms said "yes" in unison.

"Nic and Sylas, will you take Ashley as your wife? Will you love her, comfort her, honor and keep her in sickness and in health, in sorrow and in joy, and will you live for her, before all others, as long as you all shall live?"

"We will," they answered in unison.

"Ashley, will you take Nic and Sylas as your husbands? Will you love them, comfort them, honor and keep them in sickness and in health, in sorrow and in joy, and will you live for them, before all others, as long as you all shall live?"

Trembling with joy, she answered, "I will."

"Gentlemen, please face your bride, continuing to hold her hands as a symbol of your union."

She looked into Nic and Sylas's eyes and felt love bursting out of her for them.

"Nic and Sylas have written their own vows."

"I get to go first, Ethel, because I won the coin toss," Nic said.

Ashley smiled as the crowd chuckled.

"Ashley, when I look at you I am so proud and happy that you consented to be my wife. You've made me happier than I've ever been in my life. I love you. I promise that I will always be by your side, whether we have good times or bad times. I'll be there when you're sick to comfort you. And I promise that I am going to spend the rest of my life doing my best to make sure you always have a reason to smile." Nic turned to Sylas. "You're up, bro."

Once again, the crowd laughed.

Filled with emotions from Nic's beautiful words, she turned to the other love of her life.

Sylas took her hands. "You took my breath away when you walked down the aisle with Dad."

That's how I felt when I saw you and Nic.

"How could a guy like me be lucky enough to marry someone as wonderful and beautiful as you? You have made me complete. We share the same dreams and goals for our life. I promise to always be by your side no matter what comes our way for the rest of our lives. We have such wonderful examples of what our future can be right here." Sylas looked at Ethel, Patrick, and Sam. "That's what I want for you, Nic, and me. I love you, sweetheart."

Ethel smiled. "Ashley has also written her own vows."

She faced Nic and Sylas and took hold of their hands. "Wow. You've made my dreams come true. You're what I've always wanted. Two handsome, smart men. How could it get any better? I'm just so happy. I promise I will always love you and do everything I can to make you happy, whether the road ahead is smooth or rocky, whether it's sunny or stormy, no matter what we face I promise to remain beside you. I love you both so very much."

Ethel said, "Nic and Sylas, please get the ring you have chosen for Ashley."

Patrick handed the ring to Nic and Sylas.

"As you place the ring on Ashley's finger, please repeat after me. With this ring…"

Nic and Sylas placed the ring together on her hand. "With this ring, I marry you and bind my life to yours. It is a symbol of my eternal love, my everlasting devotion, and the promise of all my tomorrows."

"Ashley, you have rings for Nic and Sylas."

Phoebe handed her the wedding bands.

"Would you place them on their fingers, and repeat after me."

"With this ring, I marry you and bind my life to yours. It is a symbol of my eternal love, my everlasting devotion, and the promise of all my tomorrows."

"Nic, Sylas, and Ashley, having declared your vows in the presence of these witnesses and by the joining of hands, now, therefore, by virtue of the authority vested in me by the state of Colorado, I do now declare in the presence of those gathered that you are husbands and wife. You may kiss the bride."

"Sylas gets to go first on the kiss," Nic teased. "I lost that coin toss."

Everyone laughed.

Sylas kissed her, making her toes curl. "You're up, bro."

Nic grinned and pulled her in tight, pressing his lips to hers.

They turned and faced their friends and loved ones.

"It is with great pleasure and honor that I present to you Destiny's newest family—Nic Walker, Sylas Hayes, and their lovely wife, Ashley Walker-Hayes."

The crowd came to their feet, applauding and cheering.

Ashley marched down the aisle between her two husbands, feeling like she was on top of the world.

Chapter Twenty-Two

Nic looked at the outfit that he and Sylas had bought for Ashley to wear to Phase Four. The red vinyl skirt would barely cover her gorgeous ass. It allowed easy access to her sweet backside. The red, mesh bustier with its metal studs was perfect to show off her beautiful breasts.

Ashley was taking a bath, getting ready for the evening.

"Do you think she'll like this?" Sylas held up the skirt and top.

"I don't know if she will, bro, but you and I sure will." He put on his leather vest, which completed his club gear. After finishing Zac's final lessons, he actually felt like a Dom, inside and out. "Tonight is going to be awesome, Sylas. I can't wait to show her off on the main stage at the club."

"Me either." Sylas laced up his military boots. His Dom gear was similar to Nic's—leather pants and boots—though he wore a harness instead of a vest. "Don't get me wrong. I love the private rooms. But seeing how excited she's been since we told her what we planned to do has really lit my fire."

Nic smiled. "I was a little surprised that our wife was such an exhibitionist. Were you?"

"I sure was, but I'm glad she is. She's the prettiest sub in the whole club. I want to show her off."

Ashley came out of the bathroom completely nude, as they'd instructed her. She looked like a goddess, her skin golden and glistening.

"Masters." She got down on her knees, lowered her eyes, and clasped her hands behind her back.

He stepped forward, pride swelling in his chest at the perfection of her submissive posture. He cupped her chin, guiding her to look at him. "What state are you in, sweetheart?"

"Molten Lava Cake."

Most of the time, Ashley could only get out "Molten" during their play. By the time he and Sylas got her up on the main stage, he expected she might only be able to say the first syllable, "Molt." That image made him grin.

He recalled the day they'd chosen her safe words. He'd been so green in the life then. But green or not, everything inside him had responded to being a Dom from the very first lesson he'd taken from Zac. This life spoke to levels inside him that he hadn't even known existed before.

"On your feet," he commanded her.

"Yes, Master." She stood.

His cock responded by getting hard, but his wants would remain in check. All his focus was on Ashley. Her wants were what mattered. Once he and Sylas sensed that she was in subspace, then, and only then, would he give in to his own crushing hunger.

* * * *

Sylas put the bustier on Ashley, while Nic helped her into the tiny skirt. "Do you like your new outfit, baby?"

She smiled. "Yes, Master. I love it."

Nic went into her closet and brought out her red stilettos. "These will go perfectly, sub. Sit on the bed."

She obeyed instantly.

Nic handed him one of the heels. They each placed them on her delicate feet.

Running his hand up her legs and feeling her soft skin, Sylas felt heat pulse in his veins. He pulled his wife off the bed and into his arms.

Ashley held on tight and looked at him with her gorgeous blue eyes. "I love you, Master."

"Sweetheart, how are you feeling about tonight?"

"Anxious and excited, Sir. My molten lava cake is at least ten-feet tall."

"Just the way we like you." He kissed her. "Nic, you're driving tonight. I'm carrying our sub."

"What? No coin toss?" Nic laughed. "You got a deal, Sylas, as long as I get to carry her off the stage."

"Deal."

As Nic drove them to the club, Sylas could feel Ashley's growing trembles. "You trust us, baby?"

"Yes, Master. I trust you with my life."

He never tired of hearing her say those words. Trust. That was what the lifestyle he'd come to love was all about. He felt so confident now after completing Zac's last lesson. The uncertainty when he'd first begun learning about BDSM was gone. *I'm a Dom. I'm her Dom.*

He and Nic would continue earning her trust each and every day and night. *Especially the nights.*

* * * *

Every step Ashley took with her two Doms leading her to the main stage increased her temperature another degree. By the time she was walking up the stairs, she was on fire.

The members of Phase Four were moving to the seats in front of the stage.

They are going to watch me with Nic and Sylas. Oh my God, this is really happening.

She'd been to the club many times, but tonight was like no other. She'd never been part of a scene on any of the stages. Her first time was to be on the main one. Excitement and nervousness rolled through her. She kept her eyes locked on her Doms. They would take care of her. They would keep her safe.

As Nic guided her to the center of the stage, she heard the music that he and Sylas had selected begin to play. Tribal drums pounded out a beat that was mesmerizing, hypnotic, otherworldly.

"Dance for us, sub," Sylas commanded. "We want everyone to see how this beautiful body moves."

"Yes, Master." Her heart fluttered like mad as she wiggled her body as seductively as she could.

As she danced in place, Nic and Sylas moved next to her, touching her in places that only they knew how to touch—pinching her nipple, caressing her thigh, slapping her ass. This continued for several hot seconds until she felt relaxed and in the moment. She felt so sexy and alive.

Nic whispered in her ear. "Now strip for us. Give our audience a good show, sub."

"Yes, Master." She removed the bustier that he and Sylas had given her.

The crowd clapped and cheered their approval, which made her so happy and proud.

"They like what they see, baby. I knew they would," Sylas whispered in her other ear. "Now remove the skirt and thong but leave on the stilettos."

"Yes, Master." She knew how much Sylas loved seeing her naked with only a pair of high heels on her feet. Slipping out of her skirt and thong, she heard more applause and cheers from their audience, and that pleased her so much.

"Turn around, sub." Nic slapped her bottom. "I want to show off this gorgeous ass."

She obeyed.

"Now Master Sylas and I are going to make it pretty and pink."

Out of the corner of her eye she saw Nic pull out a paddle from his satchel and Sylas bring out a crop from his.

Oh God. Oh God. Oh God.

Sylas ran the tip of his crop up and down her back. "What state are you in, sub?"

"Molten, Master. Molten Lava Cake."

"When I count to three, I want you to grab your ankles. Master Nic is going to place his hands on your back so you don't fall when I let my crop take a bite from your sweet ass. Do you understand, sweetheart?"

"Yes, Master. I understand."

"One. Two. Three."

She bent over and wrapped her hands around her ankles. She could feel Nic's hands on her back, which shot up her desire. From this position, she was able to see the people watching them, though they appeared upside down. Of course, they weren't. She was.

Sylas ran the tip of the crop up her leg, in between her cheeks, and then flicked her ass with it. The sting that followed felt deliciously electric. Five more bites from its leather tongue landed on her cheeks, one right after another. When he began massaging her ass and rubbing her pussy, she moaned with delight. Wonderful subspace was within her reach.

He and Nic switched positions—Sylas's hand on her back and Nic caressing her ass. The slaps from Nic's paddle were different from Sylas's crop, more blunt and brutal, though just as sensual and overwhelming.

When Nic swung his paddle for the final slap, Ashley slipped into the warm, fuzzy, mysterious place that there were no words in any language that could describe it fully.

Sylas lifted her into his arms and carried her to the modified BDSM bench in the center of the stage. The leather of the bench felt cool against her ass.

Sylas and Nic placed her wrists and ankles in cuffs and attached them to the bench, restraining her spread-eagle.

"Nic, let's spin our sub around so that everyone can see this beautiful pussy." Since Sylas's first Dom lesson, he never stopped calling her pussy "beautiful."

She'd always found it odd. Pussies weren't pretty. *But in the state I am feeling now, I believe him.*

Hearing the applause, she smiled. *My pussy is beautiful.*

Nic held a violet wand in front of her eyes. "I know you like this, baby."

"Yes. Yes. Yes."

He grinned and brought the tip to one of her nipples. The spark that entered her flesh through her bud shot from her breast and all the way down to her pussy, which was dampening. The sensation that followed reminded her of a small orgasm.

As Nic continued doting her with electric kisses, Sylas pressed a vibrator to her clit.

She moaned uncontrollably.

Then she felt Sylas applying lubricant to her ass.

"What state are you in, baby?" Nic demanded.

"Molt Cake" was all she could get out.

He grinned. "I've got to have some of this sweet cream." Without another word, he began licking her pussy.

The crowd cheered and remarkably that got her even hotter.

She felt Sylas remove her restraints from her ankles. He lifted her legs with one hand.

"Take a deep breath for me, baby," he commanded. "I'm going to plug this gorgeous ass with this toy." He held it up high for her to see.

"Yes, Master." The butt plug was red, like the skirt and bustier she'd worn tonight.

"Now, let it out nice and slow."

She obeyed, willing her body to relax to accept the toy. When the last ounce of breath left her mouth, she felt him push the plug into her ass. The stretch was overwhelming, causing her to hold her breath. When the toy was all the way in her ass, her desire for more multiplied and she couldn't stop panting. She wanted her Doms inside her, needed them inside her. Just like Nic and Sylas had wanted to show her off, she wanted everyone in the club to see how great they were.

Nic removed the cuffs from her wrists. He lifted her off the bench and carried her to the Saint Andrew's Cross at the side of their stage.

Sylas pulled out a flogger with many thick tails. It was black and made of leather.

She was both in her body and out of her body, both focused and detached. Sensations rolled through her, little waves of pleasure.

Placing her with her back to the audience, her Doms reattached the cuffs to her wrists and ankles, fastening them to the cross. Then they began flogging her back and bottom.

Thud. Thud. Thud.

Each time the tails landed on her, she went deeper and deeper into subspace. She closed her eyes, riding every vibration. Bliss. Pure bliss.

Thud. Thud. Thud.

Her body burned with want.

One of her Doms removed the toy from her ass, which one, she didn't know. It didn't matter. They were her sexy duo whose synchronized lovemaking she craved.

She felt them remove the restraints. She opened her eyes and saw their naked bodies, their Dom gear piled neatly to the side. Nic moved behind her and Sylas remained in front.

"What state are you in?" Sylas's words seemed far off and yet so close, as if every syllable somehow vibrated on her skin.

"Cake. Cake. Cake. I mean…Master…"

He smiled and pressed his finger to her lips. "I know what you mean, baby. You want Master Nic and me inside you?"

"Yes, Master. Please. Please. Please."

He nodded, lying down on the bench and pulling her on top of him. His cock thrust into her wet pussy. She could feel Nic's hands on her ass, parting her cheeks. The tip of his cock pressed against her anus.

"Please, Master. I need you both inside me."

Nic pushed his cock slowly into her ass, every inch he claimed stretching her more than the toy had.

The crowd applauded, spurring her and her two Doms on. She writhed between them, filled to the max with their thick, long cocks. Their joint thrusts into her body caused the pressure inside her to build and build.

"Oh God. Oh God. Oh God."

Nic held her waist as he continued pounding her ass, again and again. Sylas thrust up into her with animalistic intensity, his hot breath skating over her neck.

She was mad with desire for the men who had changed her entire life and given her the dream she'd wanted.

When Sylas bit down on her earlobe, she could no longer hold back. The pressure released and she came. *This orgasm is like…like…Molten Lava Cake.*

She started giggling as the wild, electric sensations continued rolling through her body. She felt Nic and Sylas come together inside her and heard the cheers of their audience.

This is where I've always belonged, between them, in the arms of my loving Doms.

THE END

WWW.CHLOELANG.COM

ABOUT THE AUTHOR

Chloe Lang began devouring romance novels during summers between college semesters as a respite to the rigors of her studies. Soon, her lifelong addiction was born, and to this day, she typically reads three or four books every week.

For years, the very shy Chloe tried her hand at writing romance stories but shared them with no one. After many months of prodding by an author friend, Sophie Oak, she finally relented and let Sophie read one. As the prodding turned to gentle shoves, Chloe ultimately did submit something to Siren-BookStrand. The thrill of a life happened for her when she got the word that her book would be published.

For all titles by Chloe Lang, please visit
www.bookstrand.com/chloe-lang

Siren Publishing, Inc.
www.SirenPublishing.com

Lightning Source UK Ltd.
Milton Keynes UK
UKOW06f1933070915

258236UK00020B/500/P